MUGGED IN TAHITI

A MARINER'S TALE

Ian Verchère

New Generation **Publishing**

ALSO BY IAN VERCHÈRE

Air Transport in Crisis

The Investor Relations Challenge

East Coast Diary

ABOUT THE AUTHOR

Ian Verchère worked as a travel, aerospace and business journalist and editor in London and Hong Kong and spent several years as vice president corporate affairs for Bank of America in Tokyo and New York. His enthusiasm for boats includes sailing the waters of Chesapeake Bay and watching sunsets and ospreys over Virginia and Maryland. He was educated in Scotland, Sri Lanka and France, has two daughters, two grandsons and lives with his partner Jane in England.

In memory of my parents
Adnah and Charlie
and for the family that followed

'I cannot rest from travel; I will drink
Life to the lees.All times I have enjoy'd
Greatly, have suffered greatly, both with those
That loved me, and alone; on shore, and when
Thro' scudding drifts the rainy Hyades
Vext the dim sea.'

Ulysses
Alfred Lord Tennyson

Acknowledgments

I am indebted to my old friend and 'cultural adviser' Stewart Francis for his tireless efforts – usually despatched from somewhere between England (for the cricket) and France (*pour la cuisine*) -- at keeping my punctuation, syntax and grammar on course and, metaphorically speaking, doing so without the ease of satellite navigation but rather in the old-fashioned way: dead-reckoning and sextant. Thanks also to Judy Lockyear who offered encouragement when needed and highlighted those occasional lapses in continuity and good taste. And finally, a word of gratitude to those eagle-eyed wordsmiths – Ross Clarke in London, Ian Gill in Manila and Godfrey Scotchbrook in Hong Kong – for tempering my vanity with occasional praise.

NOTE TO READER

Most tales about the oceans of the world and the mariners and vessels that venture upon their vacant surfaces are a cocktail of fact and fiction, of truth and half-truth. This one is no exception and contains something of each. A voyage across the Pacific Ocean in a relatively small sailing vessel from the Florida panhandle to the archipelagos of French Polynesia *did* occur some years ago. And it *did* include a curious cast of characters, some of whom survived and others who did not.

For those who survived it was a voyage of adventure, truth and self-discovery as well as a catharsis of pent-up longings, bitter emotions and regrets. For those who did not – whether captains, crew or owners -- it was either a predictable end-game of mortality or professional eclipse.

As with life onshore, a long trans-oceanic passage in a sailing yacht gradually becomes a microcosm of the wider world in which some people do better than others: some are enriched by the experience and flourish; others are impoverished and fade away; some live and are fulfilled; others die and are never heard of again...

One

It was an offer he couldn't refuse. He'd be one of a four-man crew ferrying a forty-nine-foot yacht called *Bella Mama* from Fort Lauderdale, on south Florida's Atlantic coast, to Tahiti in the middle of the Pacific Ocean. The job paid one hundred dollars a day -- with no deductions for victuals or bunk -- and included air fare back from Papeete, in French Polynesia, to the point of departure.

He'd be the elder statesmen of a youthful team whose captain, Thaddeus – nickname Tad -- was thirty-two and about to embark on his first professional command. Other crew members were in their mid-twenties. From the skipper's perspective, Ewan's face fitted perfectly: he spoke Spanish and French which would be useful languages in places like Panama, the Galapagos and Tahiti. He also had a US Coast Guard captain's licence – which pleased American insurers because *Bella Mama* was on the US register of vessels – as well as a Royal Yachting Association offshore certificate and a reasonable amount of blue water sailing experience.

He was also perceived by his lanky Canadian interlocutor as 'someone who's been around a bit and can regale us with tales of things you were doing before we were born.' That part wouldn't be too difficult. The captain and his mates seemed so young. As for the sailing: *vamos a ver,* as they say in the bars of Havana.

There would be long days and nights at sea, explained Tad, when tedium sets in and the quality of conversation and narrative from the younger set palls. This was a rare occasion, it seemed, when 'age and life experience' were to be accorded some kudos. In a world of diminishing opportunities for the ageing, adventurous male something like this was unlikely to pass his way again.

There were other good reasons to accept Tad's offer. A couple of years before, while still in his late fifties, he'd been diagnosed with prostate cancer. An initial prostate specific antigen test – or PSA -- was undertaken as part of a routine health check in London which revealed a reading of 12.50 nanograms per millilitre. This set alarm bells ringing. More tests followed – including a painful Gleason biopsy – which said he was too young to ignore the symptoms. Something had to be done.

His preferred option was to do nothing. But that was too risky. Weighing the pros and cons of diminished sexuality against the risk of terminal cancer was not an easy call. Fortunately, he chose a treatment that proved satisfactory. His PSA count headed south to acceptable levels and he breathed a sigh of relief.

Later, when he asked his Jewish oncologist – the aptly named Dr Adam Dicker – at the Thomas Jefferson University Hospital in Philadelphia about an appropriate post-treatment lifestyle the advice – knowing of his passion for things nautical -- was succinct and to the point:

'Go sailing, my friend, and enjoy the rest of your life. Life is for living.'

'And what then of my glorious career and all those souls who depend on me for this and that?' asked Ewan.

'Sir,' he replied in that lazy laconic American way, 'they'll get by without you.'

Ewan loved sailing and Dicker's words rattled around his head for days. His urology oncologist's advice was right. Dicker by name, perhaps, but not by nature.

Another good reason for considering this Tahiti

offer was the state of his marriage. After a thirty-five-year partnership variously lived in Paris, Barcelona, London, Hong Kong, Tokyo and New York, his long-time soul mate had bowed out and returned to the bosom of her family in America. She wanted a calmer life away from the demands and unpredictability of his nomadic career. She'd also attended self-assertiveness seminars and fallen easy prey to the dubious voodoo of psycho-analysis and its more predatory brother, psycho-therapy. Loyalty was swept under the carpet; the family rent asunder. Against such adversity the mid-life husband had little defence. Under orders, he sold the house and stored the contents – a painful and sometimes nostalgic process – and moved into a tiny London flat. Like many separations, it would ultimately lead to a painful and bewildering divorce.

From there on life changed. He pursued his day job as a business editor and aerospace journalist on *The European*, a weekly newspaper launched in 1990 by media monster Robert Maxwell but later acquired by the tax-shy Barclay Brothers, future proprietors of *The Daily Telegraph*. Elsewhere, he toiled into the small hours of the morning on a business book about the international air transport industry which he'd been commissioned to write for the Economist Intelligence Unit. Journalistically, it was a sector he'd followed for many years. In between work on this project, there were assignments to interesting venues like South Africa, Sri Lanka, South Korea and various parts of Europe; they were, of course, therapeutic but not a solution to his tortured soul.

AFTER THREE decades of marital discipline, his new life as a middle-aged man-about-town with *pieds-à-terre* in central London became one of breath-taking emancipation. Gone were those grim commutes in and

11

out of the metropolis on appalling suburban trains. Gone, too, were the constraints and obligations of domestic life. He was transformed from *pater familias* into a laid-back, self-indulgent bachelor gliding freely between favourite pubs, restaurants and late-night wine bars.

He rediscovered a *demi-monde* of singles London, much changed from the free-parking, free-drinking, mini-skirted 1960s of his distant youth. The non-professional life was now his own to do with as he pleased. He cooked when the mood so willed; he ordered take-away dinners and ate them at ungodly hours. He watched strange television programmes at three o'clock in the morning – some educational, some less so. He took dirty clothes to the neighbourhood laundrette and chatted with little old ladies fighting to survive on Britain's niggardly state pension.

Then one beautiful spring day, as if to remind him of his own mortality, he and *The European* parted company. Andrew Neil – sometime editor of *The Sunday Times* – had been hired to rescue this ailing organ from extinction. Because *The European* was losing millions, the new owners – the hugely-rich but media-shy Barclay brothers – had brought in this Paisley heavyweight in a last-ditch but hopeless effort to save the late Mr Maxwell's experiment in pan-European newspaper publishing.

A ritual blood-letting ensued. One by one, the paper's old stalwarts and celebrity columnists like Peter Ustinov were struck off the payroll as Mr Neil out-sourced their livelihood to his freelance cronies. The format of *The European* was altered from broadsheet to tabloid and plastered with screaming headlines and virulent attacks on everything to do with Brussels and the European Union. Then, a few months later and notwithstanding its over-worked brand of investigative journalism and purple prose, the paper folded. Neil returned north of the border to edit *The Scotsman* and host late-night TV chat shows.

Prostate cancer, a faltering marriage and a redundancy cheque sent dark clouds scudding over his head. Anger and resentment consumed his soul, dulling his enthusiasm for life in the process. What had he done to warrant such an unfair package of setbacks? he asked. Quite a lot, came the response. No life or partnership was blameless. But his conscience wasn't ready for any quick-fix Faustian trade-offs. Self-doubt reigned supreme.

Philosophically, there seemed one obvious escape: rewrite the script and make a new movie. It was a cute metaphor, he reflected. But not all minds deleted at the stroke of a key. Some recycled the details and – left unattended – dragged their owners into a quagmire of despondency. Another approach was to turn such mawkish self-doubt to advantage. A nasty package had to be confronted and out-witted. Play one's cards right, thought Ewan, and life might – paradoxically -- acquire new meaning and direction.

And so one chilly day, in a mood of impulse and uncertainty, he packed his bags, bought a discount ticket to Miami and headed for the sunshine. As grey British skies receded, he sipped his first chardonnay of the day and marvelled at the technology of the big Airbus as it lurched through high cumulus into the sunshine to its pre-ordained altitude.

Europe's aerospace industry had finally caught up with the Americans in the design and production of these magnificent airliners and this big-beast A340 was part of that effort. First Lockheed and then McDonnell Douglas had been driven from the civil market by an inspired, French-led consortium of European plane makers. Only mighty Boeing – symbol of US aeronautical supremacy – now held this title in its grasp. He remembered late-night conversations in Toulouse with Airbus chief executive Jean Pierson and the Frenchman's categorical assurance that Europe would achieve his stated industry goal: to acquire at least a fifty per cent share of the world market for big civil airliners. That target was already being achieved, insisted Pierson. It was a remarkable example of what European industry could achieve if it pulled together. With these thoughts percolating through a groggy mind, Ewan drifted into mid-air reverie and was soon fast asleep.

Eight hours later, the big jet swept down over the turquoise waters of the Great Bahama Bank towards Miami International Airport. The neat suburban yards of grid-iron America flashed briefly by before the captain put his charge deftly onto the runway, engaged reverse-thrust and taxied to the terminal.

Once disembarked, he ambled along the well-carpeted walkways of this burgeoning American gateway, then cleared immigration and collected his bags from the carousel downstairs. Unlike London Heathrow's patchwork architecture and disorder, Miami's airport had a singularity of design that helped bring calm to the addled mind after a long, wine-soaked flight. He exited the building onto the sidewalk and felt the familiar humid ambience of south Florida: a cocktail of petrol fumes, fast-food aromas, drawling American accents, palm trees and the staccato rhythm of Cuban Spanish. Like southern California, New York City and parts of Texas, Florida had become a less Anglo and more Latino part of the United States. He felt relaxed and happy to be somewhere else.

Two

E wan Tulloch Carswell Marshbanks – to give him his full baptismal name – had been coming and going to and from Britain for most of his life. It began when he was two. The first excursion in 1940 was when he sailed in wartime convoy from Liverpool to Bermuda. His father – Pop – had been recruited from the Marconi Company, where he'd served as a radio officer in the British Merchant Navy, into a top-secret entity called the Admiralty Civilian Shore Wireless Service and later absorbed into Government Communications Headquarters, better known today as GCHQ. The ACSWS was an important part of the Royal Navy's attempt to harness radio direction finding (RDF) and wireless technology as intelligence weapons against German naval power during the Second World War. With its radio telephony know-how, Marconi at the time was an important recruitment pool.

Prior to their departure, Pop and colleagues had trained under cover of the General Post Office, experimenting with the practicalities of this critical new technology in the Essex and Hertfordshire countryside, north of London. If Bletchley Park's code-breakers were to unscramble Germany's Enigma submarine messages, those signals had first to be successfully intercepted. The key attribute of RDF at the time was its ability to ascertain the direction from which a radio signal was originating. Two independent recipients of the same signal employing the same type of equipment could, in theory, geometrically pinpoint or triangulate the whereabouts of the sender. This would soon prove an effective weapon against the packs of U-boats operating in the North Atlantic at the height of Germany's merciless attacks on Allied shipping.

Since U-boat commanders were under orders to

signal Berlin every twenty-four hours, a daily window of opportunity opened to detect these submarines and – depending upon the clarity of radio reception and the deployment of suitably-equipped Allied shipping – mount effective anti-submarine offensives. Initially, much of this effort depended on building a network of land stations and on equipping Royal Navy and Allied escort and patrol vessels with RDF. As part of this effort, the British Admiralty constructed a major facility at Daniel's Head in Bermuda capable of intercepting U-boat communications throughout much of the North Atlantic.

It was as part of this development that Pop, baby Ewan and his mother were despatched to Bermuda. Wives and children could accompany their men folk or remain behind in Britain. The choice was theirs. Ewan's parents – very much in love and with an 18-month old baby – opted to run the U-boat gauntlet and, if torpedoed, all die together or, God willing, continue the war against Hitler's lethal navy from an uncertain island sanctuary in the Atlantic Ocean. Given Britain's indecent retreat from the Channel Islands and their swift occupation by the Germans, the portents were not good.

Indeed, they had barely ventured beyond the Liver Birds at the gateway to Liverpool when their convoy – still forming in the adjacent waters – came under U-boat attack with the loss of several vessels. At which point their liner – the *RMS Queen of Bermuda* – struck out on its own in accordance with standing orders mandated at the time. Weeks later, after sailing through the ice floes of the Arctic Circle to avoid perilous shipping lanes and then down the eastern seaboard of North America, the liner took an easterly course and eventually sailed through a gap in the reefs into the safety of Hamilton harbour.

At the time, there were no motor vehicles in this sleepy British colony and local transport comprised either horse-drawn buggy or bicycle. And as Germany never succeeded in developing a long-range bomber capable of attacking Bermuda, Daniel's Head station played a critical and unscathed role in the detection and destruction of enemy submarines with relative impunity. During these wartime years Ewan's father led the double life of a man at one moment in an island paradise playing cricket and sailing and at another plunged into the life-and-death dramas of the Battle of the North Atlantic at one step removed.

Before entering the Second World War, the United States had signed a ninety-nine-year lease with Britain for a base in Bermuda in exchange for a fleet of ageing Great War destroyers with which to bolster the Royal Navy's dangerously over-extended convoy escorts. As Bermuda was only 568 miles off the US east coast, this meant, among other things, that abundant supplies of most kinds – including delicious American ice cream -- were flown to the island on a regular basis throughout the war. Ewan's addiction to ice cream still remained to this day which was another good reason to be in America where its consumption was serious business.

Along with other Admiralty colleagues, the arrival of the family was seen at the time by the fiercely pro-British Bermudians as an important part of the war effort and they were welcomed into their midst with great enthusiasm and hospitality. This was a particularly convivial wartime posting and one that left Ewan's parents with an enduring affection for the local populace. At the time, of course, 'locals' referred to Bermuda's white colonials who practised a mild form of racial segregation that effectively confined its former black slaves to menial and domestic work. Although he was oblivious to the fact at the time, his first school was whites-only Sandy's Grammar School, which formed part of this racial divide.

AFTER THE comfort of life in fortress Bermuda, returning to the austerity of post-war Britain in 1946 had come as a rude shock to Ewan -- for whom Britain was still an unknown country -- and his family. It was certainly enough to persuade his father to remain with the Admiralty and GCHQ as it adapted its post-war eavesdropping skills to Britain's Cold War intelligence needs *vis-à-vis* the Soviet Union and the People's Republic of China. The primary attraction to his parents – he now also had a baby-boom sister -- apart from whatever covert satisfaction Pop's job may have afforded, was that of being required to undertake overseas tours of duty, usually for periods of three years, in places where London had decided to establish strategic listening stations.

As these were mostly in far-flung corners of the British Empire where the climate was warm, spirits were cheap and the white man still enjoyed a privileged lifestyle, the attractions were not hard to fathom. After the war years in Bermuda, his parents and sister did three such tours in Ceylon (today's Sri Lanka) and one in Malta. These were separated by two or three-year home postings to any one of the Admiralty's stations in Fife, Hampshire or Yorkshire.

During the first of these post-war tours, however, it was decided that Ewan would be wrenched from the family bosom and left at boarding school in Scotland. Having become something of a wild colonial boy in wartime Bermuda, the family – encouraged by disapproving relatives in Edinburgh – decided the time had come to stamp the imprint of Scottish education on their wayward son. Kilts, porridge, bagpipes, golf, Sir Walter Scott, Rabbie Burns, Jimmy Shand, Robert

Louis Stevenson and oatcakes – to name a few random icons of the period – were to be indelibly seared on his receptive mind. In short, he was to become a Scotsman and, notwithstanding a life spent mostly outside that country, this would be how he saw himself thereafter.

As the rest of his family enjoyed the twilight years of British rule in Ceylon pampered by house boys, cook *apus*, garden coolies and *dhobi-wallahs,* "young master" battled in post-war Britain with the rigours of Scottish winters, school initiation rites, bullying, belting and grappling with the off-side rules of rugby football. An added bonus at his particular Perthshire academy was an appreciation of bagpipe music and some of its more stirring pibrochs, laments and martial airs. Coming at a particularly formative period of life, the years in Scotland represented a cherished period of cultural brainwashing of a Calvinistic variety from which he'd probably never fully recovered.

He still vividly recalled that afternoon in January 1947, during the worst winter in living memory, when he hugged his mother for the last time and then tearfully watched her drive the wobbly Austin Seven between banks of snow down the long drive through the school gates and out of his life for the next three years. In this fate, he was not alone. Only one boy in his dormitory had parents living in Scotland. All the others were either tea planters in India, rubber planters in Malaya, a diplomat in Brazil or a newspaper editor in Singapore.

Hereafter, school holidays were spent with an aunt and uncle either in Edinburgh or at their small rustic estate in the Shetland Isles or visiting his uncle's wide circle of friends on estates and farms in Scotland. On other occasions, Ewan was variously parked at a boarding house in Marchmont, as occurred over one forlorn Easter fortnight in Edinburgh, or accompanied his uncle – a notable Scottish golfer -- on golfing trips to Cruden Bay, Gleneagles, Carnoustie or Gullane on the east coast of Scotland.

There were also short but important mid-term breaks spent with his mother's sister at her flat on Blackford Hill with its sweeping vistas across the Scottish capital towards Arthur's Seat. Stricken by rheumatoid arthritis and living in more modest circumstances than her well-to-do brother, she and her family alleviated the sense of abandonment Ewan felt by his parents' departure through her warmth and affection. Memories of her gentle, pain-wracked face still brought tears of sadness to his eyes.

So, too, did he remember the day his handsome father – bronzed by three years in the tropics – came to collect him from school on his return to Britain. Sitting in the LMS train as it rattled through the beautiful Perthshire countryside and over the Forth Bridge to the Caledonian Station, Ewan experienced filial love that day as never before. The sense of relief at the return of this half-forgotten face and of being reconnected with his family would leave a deep and lasting impression.

Having analysed things more closely after their return, his parents decided that abandoning an offspring to this ethnocentric shock treatment – along with the neglect of family guardians in Edinburgh -- had probably not been such a good idea or a particularly humane one after all. Although delighted with his melodious Scots accent and ruddy cheeks, they were saddened and overcome with guilt when his house master and the school matron later described the shabby condition in which his school uniforms were sometimes returned to school after the holidays.

His wealthy Morningside kinsfolk, alas, had no children of their own; nor had they much appreciation of what was expected at a Scottish boarding school where the dress code – be it kilt or blazer - ranked high on godly virtues. If ever aware of such trifling details, they had long since forgotten the extent to which neglect of this kind exposed a bespectacled nine-year-old to the bullying and mockery that characterised British public school culture at the time.

Pity, indeed, the poor English boy whose father – a major in the British Army – had sent his son to this bastion of Scottish insularity for a superior education, little realising the burden an accent from south of the border would impose. Even at nine, Ewan's heart went out to him. Within a term, this forlorn Sassenach had acquired a flawless Perthshire accent and become an instant Scot. At the time, assimilation in the home of The Enlightenment was a ruthless but essential process and anything but enlightened. Scotland's union with England, brought about by the former's greedy eighteenth century lairds and landowners, was culturally still resented in many classrooms north of the border as it is to this day.

The net result of this hiatus in family bonding was that, when they embarked on Pop's next posting to Ceylon, Ewan was on board the Dutch liner *Willem Ruys* with his family as they sailed out of Southampton and past The Needles bound for Colombo. The sense of relief at not being abandoned for a second time was palpable. He still shuddered to think of the psychological damage inflicted on the waifs and bairns of empire dumped in boarding schools – English and Scottish – and often without parental contact for the remainder of their childhood. Mercifully, the advent of low-cost jet transport in the mid-1950s would see the gradual demise of this harsh process of abandonment as children flew abroad to rejoin their expatriate parents for school holidays and re-bonding.

Although all this meant a further interruption to his

education and an end to its Scottish dimension, it also allowed him to become re-acquainted with a family he'd almost lost contact with after Bermuda but would again come to love and appreciate all the more in the years ahead. At the same time, though, it exposed him to a pattern of departures and arrivals from his homeland which sometimes enriched and sometimes impoverished his life. It was a nomadic habit that never totally disappeared as he later studied and taught in Paris and Barcelona and then went on to accept employment in Hong Kong, Tokyo, New York and London.

Three

Ewan and his family arrived in Ceylon, today's Sri Lanka, on the day that King George VI -- still this former British colony's head of state – passed away in 1952. This was closely followed by the untimely death of the newly-independent nation's first Prime Minister, D.S.Senanayake, after a riding accident on the Galle Face Green in Colombo. As the "father of the nation," D.S. represented to Ceylon's struggle for independence from Britain what Mahatma Ghandi and Pundit Nehru did to India.

His enormous funeral procession – replete with magnificent temple elephants, turbaned Kandyan drummers, saffron-robed Buddhist monks and multitudinous mourners garbed in white saris and sarongs – made a profound impression on Ewan as it snaked its way through the teeming streets of Colombo. The glow over the city as Senanayake's funeral pyre burnt into the night, not to mention the whole notion of public cremations, was heady stuff for an impressionable youngster newly arrived from the lochs and glens of Perthshire.

This and the king's death added a rather sombre note to their first few weeks in this beautiful Indian Ocean island. But the funereal mood would give way to happier times when Ewan was plucked from the Royal Navy School in Colombo and settled into an Anglican Church Missionary School in Kandy, the pre-colonial capital of this ancient offshore kingdom. Indeed, by the time they embarked on a P&O liner for the voyage back to Britain in 1955, Ewan's life had been enriched and transformed beyond all recognition after three years at Trinity College, a replica English public school set amidst the verdant hills and tea plantations of up-country Ceylon.

At the time, Trinity was mainly populated by upper-crust Sinhalese, Tamil, Eurasian and foreign boys – often the progeny of tea planters, judges, civil servants, doctors and businessmen – which offered a unique insight into both Christian and Buddhist values, not to mention the impact of European imperialism on Asia. Over the preceding four centuries, the Portuguese, Dutch and British had all variously incorporated this beautiful island – known to the ancients as Serendipity – into their sprawling global empires.

As the last of these white aliens – or *pariah sudahs* as they were sometimes called in Sinhalese – the British left the most enduring legacy on the country through language, education, constitution and sport. Part of that inheritance remained the continuing survival and support for Christian institutions like Trinity College and its arch rivals St Thomas's, Royal, St Anthony's and Wesley schools. Not only did it give their alumni a good education, but it also facilitated their emigration and integration into richer Commonwealth nations during Sri Lanka's post-colonial period of non-alignment and cultural introspection; not to mention the brutal efforts of the Tamil Tiger secessionists to split the island along ethnic Tamil and Sinhalese lines. His time there was good training for the emerging multi-cultural, post-colonial world that this western expansion would create.

By the time they embarked for Southampton in 1955, however, he was homesick for Britain. Ceylon was neither his homeland nor was it a country where he could hope to build a future, even as an old-style tea planter. The days when a young Scot could seek his fortune as a trainee planter with companies like Lipton and Dunlop in India, East Africa, Malaya or Ceylon were ending. All over the British Empire, the white man was under notice to quit and return from whence he'd come. Having witnessed something of his countrymen's social arrogance and sense of racial superiority in Colombo as the sun set on their empire, Ewan could well understand why.

Even as a teenager, he was frequently embarrassed by the demeaning vocabulary employed by the British – notably of the English middle-class variety – towards different elements of the indigenous population. Remarkably, places like the Colombo Swimming Club and the Colombo Club were still white bastions from which non-whites were excluded ten years after independence. Such was the degree of social conditioning achieved by a century and a half of British rule.

Through a facile mix of racism and political control, Britain had dominated vast portions of Asia, Africa and the Middle East. But the Japanese defeat in 1941 of the French in Indochina, the Dutch in Indonesia and the British in Hong Kong, Malaya and Singapore had sent a clear message to Europe's colonial subjects -- notably the overseas Chinese and Indian diasporas -- that the white man and his powerful militias and mercantile systems could be defeated by an Asian nation.

When General Douglas MacArthur accepted Japan's surrender in September 1945 on the *USS Missouri*, therefore, perceptions of European invincibility among the subject races of its empires were evaporating. The new masters of the universe were the Americans whose dislike for European colonialism – along with its propensity to exclude them from imperial markets – would expedite their end. It was time for the British, the French, the Dutch and the Portuguese to pack their bags and go home...a task which they would perform with varying degrees of grace and dignity over the next half century.

EWAN'S LONGING for home was insatiable. This time his father's posting was to Scarborough, a Victorian resort on the east coast of Yorkshire, where the Admiralty had established another of its eaves-dropping stations – this one to listen in on Russia and its restless European satellites. As they journeyed north by train, every feature of the sceptred isle – its monotonous architecture, burning slag heaps, yellow smogs, rolling countryside, reeking smokestacks and beautiful girls – he observed through rose-tinted glasses. His parents, it has to be said, were less enthusiastic.

As usual, the family moved into rented accommodation – this time a 1930s semi overlooking Peasholm Park on the north side of the town – and settled into a very different way of life from that in Colombo. As he expected to be called up for National Service within the next year, education was put on hold and he took a job – his first if one discounted schoolboy potato picking in Scotland – at Rowntree's Department Store on Scarborough's high street.

Decked out in a new Burton's suit, he reported for duty one Monday morning and was promptly assigned to the radio and electrical department under the watchful eye of a certain Mr Bielby. Mr Bielby had flown Spitfires against the Luftwaffe during the war and, *ipso facto*, was a deity in Ewan's eyes. This probably had a lot to do with the fact that, back in Kandy, he'd won the school reading prize: the Royal Air Force ace Douglas Bader's biography *Reach For The Sky*.

How heroes like Mr Bielby could end up working in a department store – elegant as Rowntree's was – puzzled him at first. Later, though, he saw in him a genial individual happy to be alive and totally

26

contented with his lot. Like his father, Mr Bielby was part of that remarkable generation of men and women whose wartime greatness had increased and become more admired with the passing of time. Unlike some conflicts in Britain's chequered history, theirs was a just war that ennobled the victors and made Ewan intensely proud to be British. Even at the tender age of seventeen – and in those days to be seventeen was very tender – men like Bielby were the stuff of heroes.

That summer in Scarborough was one of his happiest. It was also a defining period in terms of how he wanted to spend the rest of his life. For weeks on end the sun shone and the weather was sublime. He yearned to be outdoors mingling with the holidaymakers who flocked to Scarborough from the grimy industrial towns of northern England and Scotland. Instead, he was trapped in a store watching day-trippers eye television sets, washing machines, kitchen units and hi-fidelity radiograms they couldn't afford. Only Scarborough landladies had the 'brass to buy,' explained Mr Bielby, and that would only be in winter after they'd 'counted their summer takings.'

Then one day, as the temperature soared and the girls donned their best summer frocks, all became clear. Work was an inescapable part of growing up and surviving, he reasoned. This much had already been expounded upon at length by his fussing parents and relatives. The real challenge was to know how to make the whole life experience interesting and avoid this awful sense of imprisonment he felt at Rowntree's. Part of the solution lay in finding a career that afforded travel, variety and interest. Insignificant as it now seemed, this sudden revelation – a sort of teenage epiphany – was an important milestone in his youthful mind.

One option, said Pop, was to follow his footsteps

into the clandestine world of GCHQ. The various arms of Britain's intelligence-gathering activities were being consolidated as the country's foreign policy commitments shrank in the post-imperial era. The conditions of employment were good and improving. Such a job opportunity he could arrange but it was not a career path he would particularly recommend. The whole British system, he explained, was riddled with Masonic intrigue and old boy networks that often promoted the inept and incompetent. Blanketed under the Official Secrets Act, it was also a work culture with little scope for redress. His advice -- invaluable with hindsight -- left Ewan determined to be independent and to resist the lure of job security afforded by a career in government service.

Memories of transiting the Suez Canal and glimpsing camel caravans making their way between the rolling dunes of the Sinai Peninsular had seemed, at the time, a vision of eternal exoticism that was already influencing his life. Any future had to be intellectually stimulating and rewarding. The tedium of being imprisoned in a department store, coupled with an already well-travelled life, taught him a great deal that sunny summer in Scarborough. Although he was only seventeen, some things were becoming clear. If you have to work, for God's sake select a career that is as interesting and enriching as possible. It was a mantra that he would embrace for the rest of his working life.

Four

After a sleepless night in a cheap motel under the noise-print of Miami International Airport, Ewan caught a northbound train up the coast to Broward Station in Fort Lauderdale. From here it was a quick taxi ride to the boat yard. Summerfield Boat Works was one of a dying breed of Florida facilities where yachtsmen could either do work on their boats or enlist the help of yard professionals. The attraction to do-it-yourself amateurs like himself was the willingness of its workforce – be they riggers, painters, fibre-glass gurus, welders or carpenters – to give free advice on how best to undertake most maintenance tasks.

Established in 1940, the yard was owned at the time by the Summerfield family who were still resisting all efforts by Fort Lauderdale's rapacious property developers and planners to transform this valuable site into luxurious riverside condominiums. Critics complained the city's planners had been hell-bent in recent years on trying to transform the city into a high-cost business centre and a base for multi-million-dollar power yachts. Part of this preoccupation with urban tidiness and wealth was a none-too-subtle attempt to force out the many yards, boat-builders and live-aboards that once characterised this former trading post and fishing port.

Summerfield, with its timber sheds and busy storage slips, was defiantly resisting all such attempts and still exuded something of the mood and appearance of that untidy, half-forgotten world. For people who liked the sight of ocean sailboats jacked on the hard in varying states of disassembly and undress and who liked mingling with the quirky types whose passion this was, here was the place to be. Tucked away in the yard's nooks and crannies, ironically, were the neglected vessels – most of them no longer seaworthy – in which many of the yard's workers lived.

In one of these Summerfield sheds floated an unmasted sailing yacht called *Yahoo* – later re-named *Contigo* – which Ewan's new partner Jojo and he had recently acquired. *Contigo* was an elegant, 41-foot, sloop-rigged vessel built by Whitney's Operations on the lower New York reaches of Long Island Sound. Designed by a British naval architect called Alan Gurney, *Contigo* was one of 25 of these Carib 41s originally built for charter work in the British and American Virgin Islands in the late 1960s and early 70s. To small-craft experts, this immediately signalled an earlier era of fibre-glass construction when boat-builders were seeking alternatives to the costly tradition of the labour-intensive shipwright and carpenter.

While ocean shipping had long since parted company with wooden hulls in favour of welded steel or – during wartime emergencies – ferro-concrete materials, smaller vessels like fishing and pleasure craft still adhered to the old technologies and materials. But increased wealth and the attendant expansion of recreational boating in the post-war period saw many small yards on both sides of the Atlantic experimenting with steel, aluminium, ferro-concrete and – significantly – fibre-glass and epoxy resin compounds for basic hull construction. *Contigo* belonged very much to the early experimental plastics of that history.

What this meant was the abundant, indulgent use of this petroleum derivative in hull construction on the assumption that -- like steel and wood -- the heavier the build the safer the vessel. The principal characteristic of these early fibre-glass boats was a rugged, almost military-grade durability. To say they were built like the proverbial brick out-house was no exaggeration. In today's world of light and sportier GPR (glass reinforced plastic) hulls and designer sailing gear, it was sometimes hard to appreciate the uncertainty with which boat builders – ever mindful of their professional reputations and integrity – approached the use of this evolving, user-friendly plastic substitute in the 1960s and seventies. Cheap, adaptable and easier to use, fibreglass would soon become the most universally accepted alternative to the ancient craft of wooden boat-building.

The Carib 41 exemplified the liberal layering of this new substance in early hull mouldings. An additional feature – mainly to reassure the then burgeoning US charter market in the Caribbean – was the concept of an unsinkable sailboat. Such a vessel was the Carib 41 between whose hefty layers of fibreglass was pumped liberal quantities of a buoyancy core – notably underneath the forward v-birth – aimed at keeping her afloat in the event of a possible sinking.

Despite these virtues – notably the over-glassing and un-sinkability -- *Contigo* at the time of purchase was a somewhat neglected survivor of its generation. For the past two years she'd become the emergency home to a West Palm jeweller whose impeccably manicured residence had been demolished by one of those frightening brush fires that add to the many other hazards of life in "the sunshine state". The poor man had been given fifteen minutes by the local fire chief to pack up and abandon his home if he and his lady partner were not to be barbequed alive on the banks of the Intra Coastal Waterway (ICW). The fire, it seems, had suddenly and dramatically executed a 180-degree change of direction incinerating everything in its path including the unfortunate jeweller's home.

Despondent over the loss of personal effects, family heirlooms and his home, the unhappy victim called a broker friend in Fort Lauderdale saying he was fed-up with the dangers of home-ownership in Florida (hurricanes and termites included) and wanted a safer lifestyle on the water. Did he have anything suitable on his books? The broker assured him that he did and within a few weeks *Yahoo* – her old name -- was sailing up the Florida coast to a marina just off the ICW near West Palm Beach where she was plugged into shore power and transformed into a floating caravan. As such, she had joined that vast and sometimes forlorn club of Florida sailboats that never go anywhere.

It was from this inglorious fate that they'd earlier rescued *Yahoo,* re-named her *Contigo* and sailed her back down the coast to the Summerfield Yard in Fort Lauderdale. And it was back to *Contigo* that Ewan headed after deplaning in Miami the previous day. Inevitably, he was confronted with a huge list of tasks after a long absence. Having paid his respects to John Lee – Summerfield's laid-back, chain-smoking general manager -- he set about scrubbing decks, removing encrusted bird droppings, refilling water tanks, checking batteries and arranging to haul the boat onto the busy hard-standing area for anti-fouling, new zincs and other chores within the next few days.

OVERHEAD, flocks of wild parrots screeched agitatedly as they soared around the neighbourhood's abundant vegetation, lofty palm trees and tidy gardens. Huge power yachts sailed past the Summerfield Yard along the New River, either heading to Port Everglades five miles downstream or upstream to hurricane-proof marinas and maintenance yards specialising in this lucrative end of the boat business.

Most of these towering superstructures displayed large Red Ensigns signaling the fact that they were registered in one of Britain's many offshore tax havens or, very occasionally, the United Kingdom itself. Typically, these offshore venues were the British

Virgin Islands, Cayman Islands, Turks and Caicos Islands or Bermuda (others could also be on the registers of the Falkland Islands, Gibraltar, Isle of Man or the Channel Islands), all proudly flagged with the "red duster." As he observed this traffic, Ewan was reminded of Britain's two-tone approach to tax evasion which had not always endeared it to central banks around the world by tolerating these dubious tax-efficient amenities. As far as Florida's upscale yards were concerned, however, anything that encouraged luxury boating was to be tolerated.

Impeccably appointed, the chromium-encrusted mini-cruise ships that plied these waters were usually owned by affluent American, Arab, British or European interests – private or corporate. Mostly, they were crewed by bronzed young people from Britain, Ireland, South Africa, Australia or New Zealand who were invariably attired in sexy white shorts, navy tops and brown deck shoes. Their credentials for such work were often acquired at one of Fort Lauderdale's maritime schools which specialised in everything from engineering and navigation to *haute cuisine* and hospitality skills. Part of this training, of course, was being tight-lipped and discreet about their owners, their guests and their movements. Security and wealth were inseparable partners.

Like executive jets, the floating apartments they crewed were generously endowed with navigational and telecoms equipment and – from engine room to galley – always in pristine condition. These youngsters were part of a moneyed, semi-professional end of the luxury yachting world and far removed from the humbler do-it-yourself domain of Summerfield Boat Works Inc. Yet all shared a common enthusiasm for boats, whether powered by sail or engine. It was the kind of employment that attracted people who understood the need for an orderly chain of command, onboard discipline and, of course, winter sunshine.

When Ewan met the young Canadian skipper offering him passage to Tahiti a few days later at Summerfield's, he was unconsciously taking the first step across an invisible dividing line of recreational sailing that separated the keen weekend amateur from the full-time paid professional. Once aware of this transformation, he would, like Tad, resolutely and proudly identify with the latter.

Five

Thadeus Wainwright had belonged to this glamorous world of well-varnished, chromium-plated yachts for most of the past decade. A native of British Columbia, he'd been raised on a remote farm west of the Rocky Mountains in a place with the unpromising name of Horse Fly. Every Monday during term-time, Tad would board the school bus that gathered farm children from the surrounding counties and become a boarder until the following Friday evening when the bus dropped him off at the cross roads half a mile from the farm.

Like many rural youngsters in that vast and under-populated country, however, he soon headed for the bright lights of Vancouver – in his case for vocational training as a chef and food manager -- just as soon as he could persuade his father that farming was not for him. Before long, it led to a series of jobs in ski resorts and, eventually, aboard capacious private yachts operating along the western shores of North America.

California was home to some of the most elegant vessels of this kind anywhere in the world. Their owners – particularly those *nouveaux riches* barons from Silicone Valley and Hollywood -- usually had a high appreciation for most aspects of hospitality, good food and fine wines. Tad, with his angular good looks and lanky presence, fitted comfortably into this world. He'd become an outstanding *chef de cuisine* and kitchen manager and his boyish air and BC brogue endeared him to owners and skippers alike.

But he was ambitious and soon realised the only way to the top of his chosen profession was through a balanced combination of hospitality and maritime skills. Having conquered one of these disciplines, he now needed to concentrate on the other. This would call for a re-ordering of his boundless energies away from galley skills to those of bridge and deck. He had to learn how to operate, manoeuvre and sail these magnificent machines. And what's more, to do so to any corner of the globe.

The owners of luxury yachts – whether power or sail – were often demanding, socially insecure people. Vessels could be instructed to re-locate to distant venues at comparatively short notice and, within hours of arrival, their crews expected to provide a full range of impeccable hospitality services to guests jetting in from around the world. Captains had come and gone, some faster than others under the remorseless pressure of such demanding bosses; so, too, had a string of glamorous hostesses. All this Tad observed from below deck. In his mind, there was no question of the practical importance of honing hospitality and maritime skills. Less clear – as he would later discover to his costs – were those leadership qualities required of a good captain.

But somehow Tad's culinary skills had survived the exigencies of this fussy world and he'd grown accustomed to what he sometimes referred to as 'the easy compliments of the stuffed belly.' But like most perfectionists, the young chef was never totally satisfied with any of his achievements – even the best of them. Equally, he was instinctively uncomfortable and sceptical about praise from whatever quarter. His father was a tough mountain farmer who had not been over-generous in acknowledging his son's accomplishments. Nor had he been unduly impressed with Tad's 'galley job as a cook and dish washer.'

As a consequence of this and a broken family background, Tad had low expectations and self-esteem when it came to any appreciation of his work. This had engendered insecurities which, even though he didn't realise it at the time, drove him to greater heights of achievement than many of his more self-assured colleagues, most of whom were crewing luxury yachts en route to some other more stable career. Subconsciously, this paternal disdain would gnaw at his soul. It seemed as if he could shrug off any successes or customer flattery about his professional skills with lofty indifference but brood in a sea of melancholia over failure.

It wasn't too long, therefore, before Tad was becoming immersed in every aspect of yacht design, construction and operation. He subsidised this activity by working in restaurants at night where he could make good money. The rest of the time, he followed intensive courses at maritime school covering all aspects – theoretical and practical – of sailing, navigation, meteorology, piloting, engineering, electronics, sail-making and rigging. He had even flown to England to take a two-week course in air-sea rescue and safety procedures at Warsash Maritime College in Southampton in conjunction with Coast Guard helicopters.

All this activity was accompanied by a constant effort at maintaining and developing contact with existing skippers and owners of large recreational boats. Like many of his generation, Tad considered networking a critical part of his personal marketing campaign and career development. He also scoured Internet websites operated by crewing agencies and, where appropriate, presented himself in person to anyone in a position to offer work aboard such vessels. And his CV – honed and polished but not always totally accurate – was liberally circulated in these circles.

Initially, the jobs were as deckhand and general factotum aboard power yachts of varying calibre. It was important, he reasoned, to learn how to operate and manoeuvre these big beasts with their immaculate Detroit diesels, twin propellers and nifty bow thrusters. Many of the bigger versions had a permanent captain and hostess -- usually a couple – who would take on extra hands to dead-head the vessel to other ports or to undertake a particular hospitality trip with owners and guests on board. Tad's deck agility and boat empathy soon became apparent and it wasn't long before he was taking stints at the helm as confidence in his abilities grew.

There was something very satisfying, he thought, about steering one of these ungainly monsters and feeling the enormous surges of power that could be summoned from below deck. With their high superstructures and light displacement, however, modern vessels of this kind could be very susceptible to wind and current and were often scorned by weekend and blue-water sailors as fair-weather toys or gin palaces. New as he was to operating boats, Tad dismissed such condescension as pretentious nonsense. He also knew there was no mileage to be gained with professional skippers by mocking their charges.

As a breed, people who make a living from captaining sea-going craft -- no matter how modest or grand these vessels may be – take an almost instinctive pride in the role they perform. This was because they inherited a legacy of respect and deference originating back in the mists of time and which society still afforded them. With his emerging sense of history, Tad realised that without such sea captains, the world would still largely comprise disparate communities scattered in unconnected disarray around the planet. Intrepid mariners had explored and made smaller the world we inhabit. And while some may have been nobler than others, mankind's historic debt to their profession resonated to this day.

In his more romantic moments, Tad liked these notions. He desperately wanted to feel that what he was doing had a historical conjunction of some kind; that he was joining an ancient tradition with relevance to both the past and the present; that his new career was not just a means of making money but that it was part of some greater and, of course, nobler calling. Sensing this enthusiasm, the captains for whom he worked were generous with their knowledge and expertise. They were often willing to share and educate this youthful deckhand and to impart tricks of the trade garnered from experience. This meant more time at the helm and, finally and unexpectedly one day, an order to dock the vessel.

Bringing any vessel – particularly a large one -- alongside jetties, into locks or other confined spaces without damaging either the local infrastructure or your own command was an important part of any captain's responsibility. The most essential ingredient, as Tad had already grasped, was remaining ultra-calm at all times during the procedure and manoeuvring the craft at the slowest speed at which its helm would respond. There was, as the captain of any aircraft carrier or super tanker would affirm, a drift speed at which a vessel no longer did what the helm requested and where the services of tugs and bow-thrusters were required to complete the task.

The skipper who raced towards his final resting place and then slammed the engine into reverse gear hoping to bring it to a halt might impress the layman and his lady; but such showmanship could have devastating consequences if the engine stalled at that critical moment. Harbour masters and insurance underwriters the world over would readily endorse that point. And Murphy's Law dictated that there were times when such things occurred, particularly with small recreational vessels. Tad was determined that, whatever else he might or might not get right on that particular day, his first major docking was going to be flawless. And so it was. The 100-foot power yacht sidled gently into place between two other vessels of similar proportions without a hitch. It was, said the skipper of the day, as if Tad had been docking boats all his life.

TAD'S FIRST serious boat job was as one of the three-man permanent crew of an immaculate 75-foot, sloop-rigged, mono-hull that looked as if it had just sailed out of the pages of *Yachting World*. The elegant lines of her Ron Holland design suggested speed and sail efficiency on deck and luxury and elegance below. Even the crew's quarters exuded a dedication to on-board comfort and designer excellence. Owned by the two partners of a highly successful California-based IT firm, she was a toy to be enjoyed for recreational, business and social purposes, they said. Additional hospitality and catering staff would be hired on an *ad hoc* basis as required. Her primary sphere of operation would be shuttling between ports and offshore islands – such as there were – along the west coast of North America. And as he soon discovered, this could literally mean anywhere from Alaska to Panama.

The skipper of this trio was a tough young New Zealander called Graham Robertson who embodied all the best traits and characteristics of his homeland. Principal among these was dependability. He had also played rugby at national level, was a good cricketer and surfer, 'pretty handy with a number three iron' and an outstanding sailor. And what's more, noted the boy from BC, Robertson had a sort of British accent that went down well on the West Coast. Tad's father, an

Empire Loyalist of the old school, would certainly approve. Tad – being unworldly and impressionable -- was instantly attracted to the skill, athleticism and social ease of his new mentor. To watch the Kiwi shinnying up the stays and straddling the mast spreaders without harness or bosun's chair, while somewhat foolhardy, impressed Tad as he'd never been impressed before. Here was a role model he felt ready to die for...

Six

The day British Prime Minister Edward Heath announced his intention of negotiating British membership of the Common Market – precursor to the present day European Union – New Zealand was on notice that it was being pushed out of the old imperial nest. For over a century, Britain had nurtured the colonisation and economic development of countries like Canada, Australia, New Zealand, South Africa, Kenya and Rhodesia through a system of Commonwealth trading preferences. What, in essence, this meant was that Britain imported mainly agricultural produce and raw materials from these fledgling nations and sent back manufactured goods and machinery of all kinds from its giant industrial base. In theory, it was the perfect circle of imperial inter-dependence driven by preferential trade tariffs between member countries.

As a consequence, Britain came to depend heavily on these so-called white dominions for a substantial proportion of its agricultural needs. Similar arrangements applied to non-white members of the British Empire like India, Ceylon, Burma, Malaya and Nigeria. For the farmers of New Zealand this meant a guaranteed market for their burgeoning output of mutton, wool and dairy produce. Its larger neighbour to the north, Australia, had developed a similar culture of economic and migrant dependence on the mother country based on a combination of agriculture and raw materials.

The Second World War and the subsequent founding of the European Economic Community, however, would radically change all this. Surrounded by Hitler's lethal fleet of U-boat submarines, all capable of wreaking havoc on imperial shipping, the

British suddenly realised the appalling degree of vulnerability this dependence on overseas food imports had created. Not surprisingly, therefore, the emphasis in the post-war period was upon agricultural self-sufficiency at whatever cost. Membership of the European Union would further shift the pattern of British trade away from its former empire towards Western Europe. And moreover, the United States – the significant ally and super-power of the age – had not been particularly partial to European imperialism and its various ramifications.

Nowhere was this change of strategy viewed with more concern than in New Zealand where economic reliance on links with Britain was almost total. Geographically remote from their roots, New Zealanders would now need to redefine their trade arrangements and develop unfamiliar skills of self-reliance and autonomy if they were to sustain their comfortable lifestyle. Apart from the traumas of two world wars, in which New Zealanders fought alongside the British in both Europe and Asia, this was the most significant revolution to impact this young nation since its founding in 1840.

Small but well endowed, New Zealand promptly set about confronting a key requirement in this re-ordered world: that of finding new markets for its agricultural produce and encouraging inward investment in its manufacturing sector. Aggressive marketing boards were created around each of the country's primary agricultural sectors -- meat, wool, dairy and wine production – as part of this drive. No longer tied to the apron strings of Mother England, the Kiwis were now free to establish trade links with any market in the world interested in importing what they had to offer. And as luck would have it, their Asian neighbours to the north were embarked upon a period of

43

unprecedented economic development and expansion.

Tad's Kiwi skipper enjoyed filling in the blanks to his crew's knowledge of the antipodes in general and New Zealand in particular: a sort of roving ambassador who seemed to love his homeland the further from it he travelled. His was the first generation to grow up in this less certain world of what he called "go-it-alone single-handed seamanship". Among other things, this meant aspiring to being better than the competition – particularly overseas competition – at anything they did whether as sailors, sportsmen, farmers or businessmen. It had created a success-driven culture among young New Zealanders to which he felt wedded.

'As inveterate travellers, we have to be more skilled, more reliable, better educated and – bottom line – more employable than our counterparts in America, Europe or Australia if we're going to work our way round the world and be noticed,' he explained.

'Because we live so far away from our western roots, most young Kiwis have an insatiable appetite to see the world and are encouraged to do so by their families. This has a twofold effect: it reminds others of our existence and it reminds us of what a great little country we come from. So, mate, when you hire a Kiwi,' he proclaimed immodestly, 'you're getting more than just another pair of hands.'

Tad spent the next four years with the Kiwi captain and his attractive girl friend. They were an impressive and highly professional couple who taught him a great deal about sailing and operating a luxury yacht. His official job title for insurance and legal purposes was that of first mate but when they operated as a threesome, he became the boat's jack-of-all-trades and general factotum. When the yacht was fully crewed, however, Tad assumed a more hierarchical and dignified role that enabled him to delegate many of his more mundane chores to lesser deckhands. On the inter-personal side, it was also more comfortable to have additional crew members on board and not be 'gooseberry' to the skipper and his girl friend.

Although much time was spent in the marina in San Diego preening, polishing and maintaining the vessel, a number of significant passages were made to places like Alaska, Baja California, Hawaii, Fiji, Costa Rica and Panama. Some of these were with the owners and their families and business friends on board and others as three-man positioning trips. Tad's knowledge and experience grew apace with each of these expeditions. So, too, did his confidence. Soon he had learnt the knack of pulling himself up the stays and moving around the mast spreaders and upper rigging like a monkey. This impressed the passengers and reinforced his image as the bold and fearless yachtsman type that he wanted to cultivate. It also gave him magnificent aerial views of the sleek hull far below as it surged forward under sail through breaking waves and provided stunning panoramas of the surrounding ocean.

On one occasion, en route to Honolulu, he climbed aloft with five cameras strung around his neck to take photographs of a passing school of whales for various members of the ship's complement. A few days later, as if to remind himself of his culinary talents, Tad produced a gourmet dinner – his *bouillabaisse* was delectable – that not only gave the onboard chef a break from the rigours of galley duty but elevated its author to superman status in the eyes of the owner's wife and his two nubile daughters. All this assertive activity, it should be noted, was undertaken with the total concurrence and approval of his Kiwi skipper. Tad was shrewd enough to know that up-staging the captain -- whether as cook, navigator or sailor – was a swift road to the exit ramp.

ONE NIGHT in San Francisco, while enjoying the company of crews from various other managed yachts at a lively local bar, Tad found himself talking to a personable South African with piercing blue eyes and blond hair. He was the paid captain of a 49-foot Hylas sloop who had recently completed a two-year circumnavigation by way of the Panama Canal to Florida. But family problems back home in Port Elizabeth meant he now had to return to South Africa and abandon this glamorous lifestyle exploring the oceans and islands of the world and was flying home via California and Australia. Did Tad know anyone who might be interested in taking over his position in Florida? Mindful of the diminutive job market he inhabited and the speed with which rumours and news can travel, Tad smiled knowingly and said he would ask around.

Next morning, having wiped away the overnight dew with chamois and sponge from the boat's pristine topside -- a daily routine he found particularly satisfying – Tad delicately raised the subject with his Kiwi skipper over breakfast to test the waters.

'Why not apply for the job?' came the reply after some moments of reflection.

'Does that mean you want to get rid of me?' said the young Canadian with characteristic insecurity.

'Not at all. But I know how ambitious and dedicated you are to succeed in this business. And after the impeccable training we've given you over the last few years, I reckon you're up to the job. Why not throw your hat in the ring mate and, if you like, I'll put a good word in for you with the Bok.'

After a restless night weighing up the security and satisfaction of his current post against the uncertainties of striking out on his own, Tad decided it was time to move on. Those demons of insecurity had to be conquered. Nothing ventured, nothing gained, he thought as he drifted into a fitful sleep. He was now well into his thirties and it was time to move up the career ladder. Next day he told the New Zealand couple of his decision and went to look for the Afrikaner. If he landed the job, this would be his first command with everything that such an assignment entailed, including more money. But more important: he had the support of his current employer – someone he greatly respected, nay, almost worshipped -- which meant he was adhering to cardinal rule number one of the job market: never burn your bridges…you may need to cross them again.

Four weeks later, after an emotional farewell at the airport, Tad was on a flight to Fort Lauderdale. The Kiwis loved the lanky guy from BC a lot and hugged him warmly on deck before loading his kitbag, surfboard and Dell Laptop into their pickup for the last time. But experience had taught them that ships' crews, especially those employed in the volatile world of super yachts, were in a constant state of flux. It was a profession that attracted individuals of a fiercely independent, adventurous and somewhat rootless nature. It also attracted the lonely and damaged progeny of unhappy families.

'She'll be right, mate,' they assured Tad for the umpteenth time.

'And if you fuck up big time, you can always come back and be our underpaid galley slave again.'

They all laughed heartily and, for a brief moment, felt an immense affection for one other. Their friendship over the past few years, said Robertson, had been a *ménage à trois* without the sex.

'Or at least that's what I've been assured by my crew.'

They laughed and embraced warmly. In an uncertain world, they would all look back on these years together with particular nostalgia. Sipping his in-flight orange juice, Tad wondered if he had done the right thing; if the life ahead would be as fulfilling as the one he'd left behind. His stomach churned. In the months ahead such thoughts would percolate through his mind with increasing and persistent regularity.

Seven

Thaddeus knew nothing of the upheavals afflicting Ewan's personal life. He was far too engrossed in preparing his boat for the long passages that lay ahead to regard crew candidates as anything but compliant pieces to fit neatly into his planning jigsaw. At night, when he wasn't wooing his Brazilian lady friend, Maria-Dolores, Tad pored over charts, tide tables and historical weather data in an effort to predict the conditions they might encounter. Some of these findings were fed into a laptop computer to form the basis of a route and sailing itinerary from Fort Lauderdale to Papeete.

Occasionally, they were forwarded to the owners in Illinois as planning updates. This was Tad's first captaincy and he was determined to impress them with his organisational skills. On other occasions, though, he whiled away long hours playing computer games. His favourite one was a flight simulator with scary approaches over the dense high-rise tenements of Kowloon onto Hong Kong's old Kai Tak Airport. The flight path over Green Island towards Checker Board Hill set his pulse racing as his imaginary jet banked sharply to starboard and lined up on the world's most famous geopolitical runway. A successful landing was greeted by whoops of self-congratulation; an aborted one with muffled curses.

Like many of his generation, Tad defined most things in terms of success or failure. His was a highly competitive world of winners and losers. Trying to put his fantasy jetliner neatly on the thin ribbon of tarmac that extended into the harbour from Kowloon Peninsular towards Lymun Gap was a nightly ordeal to which he subjected himself. For the captain of a big passenger jet, he said, there was no room for failure.

That was how it would be on the Hylas. Haunted by the demons of his past, Tad desperately wanted to be a winner.

He and Ewan had first met one Monday morning when Summerfield's yard manager ordered him to raft *Contigo* alongside a spit-and-polish sloop called *Bella Mama*. When the yard got busy, vessels were frequently shuffled from one docking spot to the other as they arrived from down river and were processed towards the travel lift bay to be hauled out of the water onto the hard-standing area. Summerfield had a limited number of storage slips in its western basin plus a few more next to its main work shed. There were others under its row of covered sheds but these were designed mainly for the storage of power craft. Some sailing yachts, with masts stepped, also occupied these facilities.

Pat, the lift operator, and Ted, his mate, would position the big mobile travel lift over the haul-out slip where the next boat waited to be plucked from the water. Once in place, two huge belts were fed under the floating vessel's hull -- fore and aft of the keel -- and then slowly pulled upwards. Gradually the slack was taken up on the belts and the vessel lifted out of the water. As this occurred, the owner was usually on hand to examine the boat's dripping bottom. For some owners this could be an anxious moment, particularly if they had recently run aground somewhere along Florida's notoriously shallow inland waterways or had struck some unidentified rock or hard object in their travels.

Another concern, once the bottom had been pressure-hosed, scraped clean of barnacles and dried, was to see if blisters had appeared since last the vessel was hauled. Blisters on a hull were often the first tell-tale signs of a notorious fibre-glass Achilles heal:

osmosis blisters and de-lamination. If not lanced, ground-out, fastidiously dried and re-built with sheets of fibre-glass fabric soaked in epoxy resin, these blisters could portend a gradual saturation of the hull below its waterline. Like a cancer, osmosis could spread and accelerate the de-layering of the fibre-glass materials from which it was moulded and often sounded the death knell of many a fine vessel. Repairing osmosis-afflicted yachts – particularly those with less DIY-skilled owners -- generated a good income for the yard and its workers; but even a hint of osmosis could seriously damage the re-sale value and reputation of a vessel.

As the Monday morning shuffle began on that brilliant Florida morning, *Contigo* was gingerly moved into position alongside Tad's spotless new command. Handlers jumped aboard *Bella Mama's* pristine decks and attached the newcomer's lines to suitable cleats. Fenders were cautiously put in place to safeguard her hull against any markings by this shabby new arrival. Then, as the level of activity intensified, a head emerged from below deck into *Bella Mama's* centre cockpit followed by the slim shape of a sinewy, half-dressed torso. In the body's left hand, a stainless steel coffee mug emitted clouds of steam into the bright early morning sunshine.

'Steady as she goes, guys,' said the body. 'This is a million bucks worth of real estate you're manhandling.'

Ewan reached across the stanchions and proffered a hand as compensation.

'Greetings,' he said. 'Sorry to encroach on your space but I'm just obeying orders, you understand.'

Bella Mama's master grasped his hand with vice-like intensity and gave it two well-defined shakes.

'Hi, the name's Thadeus, professional captain. Welcome to the better end of Summerfield's. What are you doing this evening?'

'Nothing special,' he replied.

'How about cocktails on *Bella Mama* at six...my treat...only beer, wine and rum available?'

Ewan nodded acceptance with a willing smile.

'Ciao then. See you later.'

With that the body disappeared below deck to the air-conditioned comfort of its cabin and the bronzed, shapely contours of its Brazilian girl friend.

Cocktails on *Bella Mama*, as the sun set in a blaze of orange over an elevated section of Interstate 95, turned out to be relaxed, witty and convivial. The repartee sparkled on all sides, mainly revolving around the subject of stuffy Brits and old men (like Ewan) who ought to be locked away in one of Florida's ubiquitous retirement homes rather than trying to sail an elegant vessel like *Contigo*. Despite the cheeky style and irreverence, the vibes were good and grew better as the evening wore on.

Later, over a *filet mignon* and an excellent Australian shiraz, Tad explained that he was preparing *Bella Mama* for a passage to New Zealand. The owners would join her in either Tahiti or Auckland and wanted her positioned in time for the America's Cup. He might be looking for crew. Would he be interested? Ewan hesitated and assumed an air of bemused detachment. But his heart raced.

'Come on,' urged Tad, 'we need an old fart like you to entertain us when we run out of youthful bullshit...especially someone who speaks languages. I've no idea how much English is spoken in some of these places we're going to.'

BY DAY, Tad worked assiduously above deck overhauling the vessel's rigging. A key feature of this effort was the installation of a self-furling mechanism to simplify the raising, lowering and reefing of the mainsail. As this involved modifying a conventional mast by retrofitting a secondary track along its length and replacing the horizontal boom with a Profurl system, Tad sub-contracted this specialist work to the yard's riggers. But he irritated the Summerfield employees by fussing over every detail of the work in progress. Already there were worrying signs of an inability to delegate. To curb this need for control, he washed and wiped the boat's spotless fibre-glass decks with any one of six chamois cloths earmarked for this task – each one neatly rolled into its own particular plastic tube -- with obsessive regularity. In this way, it seemed, Tad was able to suppress his natural tendency to interfere.

'So what do you say to my offer?' he asked Ewan over a beer one evening. 'It'll be a fantastic trip and you'll get paid for the privilege.'

His angular features and youthful good-looks appealed to the older man's jaded spirits. He had the bearing and poise of a young man who knew his business and wanted to make this delivery the trip of a lifetime. And he enjoyed sailing with good sailors. Having confidence in a captain who wanted to take you half-way round the world was important. A young couple – Chuck and Nicola – would be the other crew members, he explained.

'They're old friends of mine from BC. Typical west coast types. Health freaks but damn good sailors.'

He tried to envisage living aboard a 49-foot sailboat for months on end. Did he have the physical and mental stamina to survive? he wondered. There were duty watches around the clock; there were galley tasks – catering on the hoof – to be performed in all manner of weather conditions; there were deck chores that included setting and trimming sails by day and night and in all weathers; there were bilges to be pumped when the hull started to leak; there were two engines to operate and service, one for generating power and the other to refrigerate food as well as propel them through the water; there was also a water maker whose complicated workings had to be mastered if they were to have water for drinking and the occasional shower; and, inevitably, there were the many unforeseen failures – human and mechanical – that form part and parcel of life at sea aboard a small vessel.

A few days later, out of the blue, Tad handed him a sheet of paper to read and sign. It was a delivery contract confirming his role as crew "for the delivery of *s/y Bella Mama* from Fort Lauderdale, Florida to the Tuamotu Archipelago in French Polynesia via the Panama Canal, Galapagos and Marquesas," it read. "This is a 5,700 nautical mile working delivery lasting approximately eight weeks beginning around February 25 and finishing approximately April 25. The salary is US$100 per day including on board expenses, entry permits, visas and bonds and airfare to and from your country of origin." Then, at the end of the document, the clincher: "I genuinely hope that this letter will assist you in making the arrangements to join me for this journey."

Any doubts in Ewan's mind were swiftly dispelled, particularly when he considered the alternatives. This was an offer that was certainly preferable to wintering in dreary London and hanging out with all those ageing philanderers with whom he occasionally consorted. Friends, of course, were important, especially as one grew older. But some friends aged faster than others and had little spirit of adventure. Indeed, some had been old all of their lives and seldom strayed far from home; which, in a strange sort of way, was part of their attraction to the dedicated rolling stone. This was not necessarily a criticism, he told himself, just an observation about the ageing process. There was a time in life for friends and a time for something challenging. *Carpe diem*, old fart, before the sun sets and the body from BC changes its mind.

'Count me in, Tad.'

Ewan sipped a Michelob Light and dipped into a plate of sushi nibbles on *Bella Mama*'s chart table.

'What did you say the rate was?'

'One hundred US a day,' he confirmed with a smile. Tad extended his hand and they closed the deal; then he signed the contract and handed it back to his new boss.

As always, the voice from within – the over-cautious, risk-averse Scot – started questioning the decision almost before it was taken. Dear God, what have you done? he asked himself. But Doctor Dicker, his Jewish prostate guru in Philadelphia, had told him to go sailing and enjoy the rest of his life. You've made your decision, said the inner self. Now live with the consequences. He slept well that night and dreamt of palm-fringed atolls and Polynesian maidens. Already he felt twenty years younger…

Eight

A few days later, Chuck and Nicola arrived from Vancouver. Nicola turned out to be a feisty red head who immediately began interrogating the captain about *Bella Mama*'s hull design and speed, fixed rigging and sailing aids. Her husband Chuck was more reserved and seemed eager to show deference to the captain. But neither had been to Florida before and were both anxious to dump their rucksacks and go sightseeing. All three departed in Tad's car and didn't return to the boat until late that night.

Meanwhile, Ewan wandered back through neighbourhood houses to *Contigo* which was docked in a nearby canal and continued with a list of tasks for completion before their departure in a couple of days. As the hurricane season might begin during his absence on the Tahiti trip, her deck fixtures had to be stripped to a bare minimum. This meant removing the sails and dodger as well as other on-deck items like the Avon dinghy and its outboard engine. It also meant strengthening dock lines and making anti-chafing arrangements.

Early next morning Thaddeus led his fledgling crew to a nearby school playground where he subjected them to a vigorous bout of physical exercises and sprints. Fortunately, having completed a few half-marathons in recent years, Ewan was reasonably fit; which was just as well because his future shipmates were thirty to thirty-five years younger than he was. And he most certainly did not want to feel physically inferior to these young Turks. This was a notoriously ageist generation with little respect for their elders in the workplace. He could probably expect no mercy, therefore, if they needed to subsidise or compensate for him in any way.

Being older and more worldly-wise than these youthful *matelots* also had the additional risk of creating other problems down the line. Youth can be very insecure in the presence of experienced seniors. This would be a long voyage where getting along with shipmates was a critical part of the process. A short day-sail or even one lasting a week was a finite activity with a convenient escape route for prima donnas unable to accept the brusque commands of a no-nonsense skipper. But setting sail for Tahiti as professional crew was a totally different proposition altogether. Here authority -- whether in hierarchical, professional or commercial terms -- resided firmly in the hands of the captain.

By the time they cast off and motored down the New River to Fort Lauderdale, therefore, Tad had already assumed a commanding air. At each of the five lift-bridges en route to the municipal anchorage at Las Olas Boulevard, his crisp communications on VHF radio with the bridge keepers suggested confidence and authority. Along the winding waterway they passed an impressive inventory of opulent homes and leafy gardens on both banks. This was well-appointed Florida real estate where pseudo Hispanic architecture predominated and the only thing missing was people.

Someone had explained to Ewan that the absence of human beings was due principally to an over-dependence on air conditioning, the power of television or, in a lot of cases, absentee landlordism. The exceptions were the ubiquitous Mexican gardeners -- most of them underpaid illegal immigrants -- and the occasional set-piece cocktail party where well-tailored Anglos seemed more like characters from the pages of *The Great Gatsby* than Fort Lauderdale gentry on a Thursday evening.

They floated by acknowledging the occasional wave

from passing vessels until reaching the point where the New River meets the Intra Coastal Waterway (ICW), then followed its northerly route for half a mile to the anchorage and attached a forward line to one of the city's white mooring buoys. From here, the ICW was an 850-mile coastal passage north that meandered along a mainly inland route from Miami in south Florida to Norfolk in Virginia. It was popular with American and Canadian boaters -- sail and power -- although its well-marked channels were often no more than ten to fourteen feet deep. Las Olas was a convenient stopover on the ICW for yachts heading north or south or, in some cases, eastwards out of the port's coastal inlet for the Bahamas. Tad's plan was to have a farewell night on the town followed by an early morning departure. But then things began to change...

At Summerfield's, *Bella Mama* had been connected to shore power. Once this link was removed, however, the boat's electrical system depended on two of the vessel's sources: a generator and the main engine's alternator, both diesel powered. Tad fired up the generator which burst into life but failed to produce any electricity. Since the generator produced the mains voltage that powered the deep freeze system for long voyages -- such as the one on which they were about to embark -- it was a critical part of the vessel's operating systems. Two hours into their great odyssey and it had broken down already. A worried look crossed Tad's face.

Next morning a mechanic was summoned. His diagnosis: the generator's armatures and copper windings "are shot". They needed to be completely rewound and the entire generator overhauled. It would take at least a week for a specialist firm to complete this task.

The sense of anti-climax was palpable. Tad reacted

by removing all crew members from the payroll and granting a week's shore leave.

The Passage To Panama

FLORIDA
Bimini
Ft Lauderdale
Miami
Nassau
Highbourne
BAHAMAS
Cat Is
San Salvador
Rum Cay
Long Is
Crooked Is
Acklin's Is
Havana
CUBA
Guantanamo
CAYMAN
WINDWARD PASSAGE
HAITI
Port Antonio
JAMAICA
NICARAGUA
Caribbean Sea
COSTA RICA
Colon
Panama City
PANAMA
Pacific Ocean
COLOMBIA

Nine

At nineteen hundred hours on Wednesday the thirteenth of March they cast off the municipal buoy at Las Olas and headed south down the ICW towards the towering elegance of the Seventeenth Street Bridge that separated the Port Everglades turning basin from Fort Lauderdale's residential waterways. It had taken six days to sort out the generator and *Bella Mama*'s crew were impatient to be underway. Already they were one week behind schedule. Inside the port, lofty cruise ships were neatly berthed end-to-end along the extensive docks. At the time, Port Everglades and Miami, thirty miles down the coast, handled most of the world's burgeoning cruise traffic, much of it flown in from elsewhere in the Americas and Europe.

The crew focused on tending the lines and stowing the dinghy and fenders. Tad pointed the bow east and they motored down the short entrance channel towards the open sea on the first leg of the 6,000-mile voyage to French Polynesia. Behind them the skyline of Florida's high-rise architecture stood out against the fiery orange of a setting sun. This was the last they would see of high-rise urban dwellings until Panama City in Central America. Ahead the *lapis lazuli* waters of the Gulf Stream beckoned and dolphins frolicked across their bows.

The Gulf Stream was a significant warm-water current not to be taken lightly, explained Tad. Originating in the Gulf of Mexico, it turned north at Cuba and glided up America's eastern seaboard between the Bahamas and the Florida panhandle before bouncing off Cape Hatteras across the North Atlantic. At its axis, the Gulf Stream between Florida and the Bahamas could move at anything up to four knots on its constant northerly passage. Sailing across its path, therefore, called for corrective navigation if a particular point was to be reached on the other side. This could be anything up to seventy degrees on the compass depending on a vessel's speed-over-ground, wind strength and the whereabouts of the current's axis. Plotting an easterly course of, say, ninety degrees could sometimes require setting a compass course of one hundred and sixty degrees to offset the Gulf Stream's flow. After centuries of scouring by this relentless current, the ocean here was very deep; it was also very popular with recreational anglers – or sport fishermen in Florida-speak – who fished these waters in pursuit of big game species.

Another important consideration when crossing the Gulf Stream to the Bahamas was wind direction. As most sailors were aware, wind against tide could generate unpleasant sea states. A strong twenty-to-thirty knot northerly against the Gulf Stream's four-knot movement in the opposite direction could concoct bizarre and grotesque surface shapes that made for uncomfortable (sometimes dangerous) sailing conditions and were best avoided. When continental northerlies occurred during Florida's otherwise idyllic winter months, therefore, the sport fishermen rarely ventured more than a few miles offshore...if at all. North America's East Coast sailors – power or sail – often considered their first Gulf Stream crossing to the Bahamas as an upgrade from the status of amateur day-sailor to ocean apprentice.

They were lucky that night because the wind, like the Gulf Stream, was coming from the south at about fifteen knots. But mindful of time lost, Tad decided to motor-sail and attempted to fire up the Yanmar diesel engine. The starter engaged and then whined into inertia. A second attempt and there were signs of a less-than-perfect action. The third shot started the engine but left them with an uneasy feeling of unreliability.

'We'll install the back-up starter when we get to Nassau,' Tad reassured them.

The oil pressure gauge was also giving erratic readings.

A course was plotted for North Rock on the north-west edge of the Great Bahama Bank. The North Rock lay just north of Bimini, a tiny group of Bahamian islands once very much at the heart of local smuggling, wrecking, piracy and deep-sea sport fishing. In earlier, bawdier days, Bimini was also a favourite hangout of the writer Ernest Hemingway, whose affection for big-game fishing and brawling in its shanty bars was legendary in the early post-war years.

They sailed into a star-lit night as the flickering lights and urban glow of south Florida's Atlantic coast receded over the horizon. Ewan's first stint on the helm was from midnight to two in the morning. He took over and familiarised himself with the navigation aids – compass, Global Positioning System (GPS) and the two autopilots – and steered one-sixty degrees compass for an actual bearing of one-hundred and eight degrees towards North Rock.

Tad stayed on deck for a while and then disappeared below to get some sleep. He occupied the spacious forward state room normally reserved for the owners when they were on board. Stacked neatly along the port side of the wide bunk were his newly-acquired surf board and wind-sail accoutrements. The night was dark ahead with a few stars and pulsating aircraft strobes above. The moon had not yet risen. Far south on the forward starboard quarter, the distant lights of a vessel commanded attention. The running lights suggested it was over a hundred feet long and converging on their easterly course…but not for some time.

In good weather, night sailing often had the

advantage of revealing the presence of other vessels more clearly than in daylight. In these Florida waters they usually took the form of tankers, bulk carriers or container ships steaming at twenty knots – or about three times the speed of a sailboat -- and plying northwards from the Panama Canal, the Gulf of Mexico or Miami. With additional impetus from the Gulf Stream, this particular ship's speed over the ground – which was its true speed as opposed to its speed through the water – was probably close to twenty-five knots. As with elephants in the jungle, therefore, the best strategy for small craft was to give such fast-moving giants a wide berth regardless of maritime etiquette. Normally, the speed differential saw the freighter move swiftly across the bow. If, on the other hand, the relative position of the big ship appeared to remain unchanged then both vessels were probably on a collision course and one or other – usually the yacht -- needed to alter direction.

Cruise ships -- of which there were many in these parts -- were easier to spot after dark. This was because they would light up like Christmas trees and their speed and direction become relatively easy to calculate. There was also the distant sound of music and, on occasions, the down-wind aroma of gourmet cuisine to signal their presence. However, cruise ships did sometimes have the disconcerting habit of drifting at night – or, heaving to – so as to time their arrival at the next port of call for breakfast. And there was something a little eerie or *Marie Celeste* about sailing past a seventy-five-thousand-ton, multi-decked floating palace going nowhere at three o'clock in the morning.

Like the English Channel, there were also ferries and other recreational vessels to contend with. However, most of these operated in daytime and their presence was less frequent. Sailboats like *Bella Mama*, on the other hand, often preferred to make the fifty-mile crossing from Florida at night so as to spend all the following daylight hours crossing the Great Bahama Bank. Like the Gulf Stream, this giant sandbank was a significant feature of any passage to Nassau, the main port and capital of the Bahamas. Unlike the Gulf Stream, however, its waters were rarely more than twenty feet deep and exuded an inviting translucent calm. It also had the unusual characteristic of being an expanse of ocean where sailors could drop anchor beyond sight of land and swim or fish off the stern.

Ten

They located the North Rock light just before dawn and sailed onto the Great Bahama Bank. As they did so the depth-sounder blinked back into life and informed them their depth was twenty-five feet. This was to be expected and in accordance with the charts. Above one hundred feet, this instrument no longer gave a dependable reading. The depth-sounder was an important piece of kit for any vessel undertaking coastal passages, particularly when approaching or departing unfamiliar anchorages. It also had the added benefit of being a navigational aid when linked to depth lines on charts. Its transponder – or transmitter – was located on the vessel's bottom and bounced a signal off the sea bed to calculate depth. Should a passing vessel or school of fish disturb a sandy bottom, however, depth readings could go haywire and panic an inexperienced helmsman into believing he or she was about to run aground.

By mid-morning they were twenty miles onto the bank. The sea was calm and inviting; the sky was blue; and the sun was warm. Then suddenly and without warning of his intentions, Tad cut the engine, threw two fenders over-board and proceeded to strip naked. Chuck busied himself with imaginary rope chores. Nudity was not his thing, particularly other people's. Nicola immediately turned a deep shade of red that matched her flowing locks and freckles. For his part, the senior crew member looked on somewhat bemused. As Tad removed the final item of clothing – striped jockey shorts – all eyes boggled at his amazing mid-rift. His ample genitalia languished at the epicentre of a remarkable pattern of dragons, serpents and mermaids that encircled his waist in what he later called his Polynesian tattoo. In a blinding flash of white buttocks and flailing limbs, he leapt overboard and headed for the floating fenders which were attached by line to a stern cleat.

'Come on, you wankers,' he commanded from afar, 'get into the sea.'

After some hesitation, his crew dutifully stripped off and obeyed orders. Nicola, for her part, disappeared below deck and re-appeared attired only in bikini briefs. Her well-shaped breasts received a chorus of male approval while Chuck dived under water in another determined effort to be somewhere else. Although unexpected, Tad's plunge broke the ice and engendered a welcome sense of bonhomie amongst the crew.

After a revealing dip, Nicola -- only recently married to Chuck – was soon dressed and below deck kneading dough and baking bread in a pressure cooker. Tad, in sarong, pored over charts. The Yanmar turbo-charge purred at 2,600 revolutions per minute and sounded healthy…for the time being.

The skipper had embarked on this voyage equipped with a limitless supply of pop rock CDs that would pretty much dictate the mood music on board *Bella Mama* from here to Panama City. The boat's stereo system boomed to the wailing lamentations of another broken-hearted West Coast lover. Tad generally took his daily intake of this decibel therapy in the mornings with strong coffee or, on any other occasion during the day, when he was feeling low and insecure. At present the weather conditions couldn't be better: a gentle four-knot breeze from the south-west and a sea state like glass. The rock bands stayed silent.

By fifteen-hundred hours they were coming off the Great Bahama Bank close to Chub Cay and sailing back into deep water. A small bird – species unknown – hitched a ride and investigated every nook and cranny of the boat. They fed the fearless little chap crackers and water while the crew dined on salad and Ryvita crisp bread. Later, they entered the deep waters of the Northwest Channel and sailed down the east coast of Andros Island into another inky night. A thirteen-knot northwesterly filled the mainsail and genoa and hastened their approach to Nassau. By early morning, they sighted the enormous Paradise Island Hotel – a pink tourism carbuncle that brought jobs and money to the local economy -- on the approaches to New Providence Island and the Bahamian capital.

Efforts to fire up the engine after a long period of sail-power indicated the starter was still not right. And to add to this problem, the Yanmar was over-heating and no raw water was coming from the exhaust cooling system astern. Coupled with the earlier maintenance work that had been done in Fort Lauderdale, *Bella Mama's* technical profile was not looking good. They docked at Nassau Yacht Haven, beyond the arching link bridge, and tried unsuccessfully to purchase a new crank battery which Tad felt might be the source of the problem. After only two days into this trans-Pacific odyssey, the crew's perception was increasingly one of a vessel whose engine systems were in anything but good shape. But, said Nicola, they were probably being alarmist...

LIKE MOST of the Bahamas, Nassau was once a notorious haven for piracy and smuggling. In the archipelago's labyrinth of cays, islands and anchorages, English and French buccaneers would lie in waiting for Spain's treasure-laden galleons as they sailed up the Florida coast aided by the Gulf Stream's northerly flow. English pirates stealing from Spanish looters, as it were. Today, it was more a sanctuary for North American, British and Latin American tax exiles and, on some occasions, questionable business deals. *Plus ça change…*

Gun runners, rum runners, people traffickers and drug cartels had all variously used its convenient geography and malleable residents to their advantage. These civic delinquents eventually morphed into a ruling oligarchy of mostly white Bahamians called the Bay Street Boys – a motley band of merchants, accountants, lawyers, politicians and local businessmen -- who ran these disparate islands like a private fiefdom and effectively suppressed the black majority under a code of segregation and racial prejudice like that once practiced in the southern United States. Their stranglehold was finally broken, however, with the arrival on the Bahamian political stage of a black, London-trained barrister by name of Lynden Pindling.

In the nineteen-sixties, Pindling successfully marshalled the majority black electorate behind his Progressive Liberal Party and seized political power by popular vote, leading to the country's full independence from Britain in July 1973. Since then, most of the Bay Street Boys had taken their assets elsewhere and the Bahamas become just another former British colony living comfortably close to the United States and generally enjoying a higher living standard than its Caribbean counterparts further south.

Historically, however, the United States had often been on the receiving end of the former colony's more nefarious enterprises. After independence from Britain in 1973, for example, the use of the Bahamian island of Norman's Cay in the Exumas by Colombian drug trafficker Carlos Lehder – co-founder of the notorious Medellin Cartel -- as a staging point for airlifting narcotics into Florida set alarm bells ringing in Washington. Denials of complicity by Pindling and his newly-independent government did not impress the

Americans. As a result, the Bahamas was now independent in name only and its waters – unofficially – were closely monitored by the United States Coast Guard and the US Navy's eagle-eyed satellite surveillance systems.

Notwithstanding its black majority, the Bahamas still condoned a tenuous form of white racism in places like Lyford Cay – a gated community of international tax refugees on the west end of New Providence Island with its own schools, stores, marinas, golf courses and exclusive amenities – where inmates buy Bahamian residency and the presence of locals is discouraged. There is no income tax in the Bahamas which appeals to its wealthy offshore exiles.

Having read up *The Lonely Planet* guide on the Bahamas, the young Canadian couple made a quick tour of Nassau after which *Bella Mama* sailed eastwards past Porgee Rocks and set course for Highbourn Cay, forty miles southeast of New Providence Island. She sailed into inky darkness ahead and star-studded heavens above and was backed by a fifteen-knot north-westerly. The boat's backup starter was installed en route but still failed to fire the engine. Shortly after midnight, they dropped anchor off Highbourn, a small island at the north end of the 180-mile chain of Exuma Cays. Ewan ate a bowl of cereal, checked the anchor lines and crashed for a good night's sleep.

Eleven

They woke next morning to find themselves in an idyllic setting of turquoise waters, white sands and three low hills, one of which was surmounted by a lofty telecoms relay mast. Leroy – a local fisherman – sidled alongside *Bella Mama* and, after some good-humoured badinage, sold them three hefty lobsters at ten dollars each from the bottom of his boat. Tad – *le chef* – boiled one and turned it into a rich lobster omelet.

'We'll cook the other two and have them later with buttered rice and garlic butter,' he said.

They exercised their bodies swimming round *Bella Mama* several times and then – after toweling down – set about trying to find out what ailed the starter system. Aided by blueprints and electrical block diagrams, Tad and Chuck trouble-shot their way to the battery isolator switch, thinking they might have found the solution …they hoped.

Ewan's mind wandered to thoughts of Jojo – his soul mate and partner back in England – and he regretted she was missing all of this. The setting was perfect. He tuned the pocket radio to Radio Havana and tested his command of Spanish. Cuban Spanish was often easier to understand than the Mexican variety prevalent throughout much of the United States. This was, he reminded himself, one of the reasons the skipper had hired him: as his official interpreter. He listened to a barrage of anti-American news reports attacking the activities of Cuban exiles in Florida. As more Castro ideology crackled over the air waves, he felt happy to be part of this youthful, if somewhat unworldly, crew.

The young of today may seem political *inocenti* – or perhaps just politically indifferent – but they knew far more about healthy eating, lifestyle issues, gender politics and robust exercise than his generation ever did. Their focus was much more on ideas to do with conservation, environment, interpersonal relations, multi-culturalism and understanding and protecting planet earth. The rigid ideologies of state ownership versus capitalism that once preoccupied Ewan's post-war generation – nuclear disarmament and the anti-apartheid movement – were long gone. Today's youth, it seemed, were more concerned about the pros and cons of globalisation, electronic gadgetry, fashion, brand names and conspicuous consumption. All of which kept the capitalist machine running smoothly on its mindless journey. Or so it seemed at the time. What a pity they couldn't coax this delinquent Yanmar down the same path.

After a pasta salad prepared by Ewan, they upped anchor and motored through the cut – nasty rocks on both sides – into the deep waters of Exuma Sound and set a course of one hundred and fourteen degrees for Hawk's Nest on Cat Island. Their unpredictable engine seemed to have been cured for the time being by a hefty blow to the starter's solenoid fuse.

'Solenoids sometimes need a kick up the ass to make them do their job,' said Tad after long hours of fruitless trouble-shooting.

At zero-three-fifteen hours, the skipper made them an early breakfast of scrambled eggs and cold potatoes and relieved him from the Dog Watch. The food was welcome but not up to his usual epicurean standards. They beat into a southeasterly wind for the rest of the night and then – around noon -- entered a narrow channel and motored to the Hawk's Nest fuel dock. Hawk's Nest was a tiny, away-from-it-all island resort with a small landing strip and sandy beaches; the perfect refuge for wealthy US mainlanders arriving by private aircraft or boat that provided fuel, cottages, fishing, tranquility and a pleasant anchorage.

But once they'd docked, Tad proceeded to abuse the dock master for having summoned the local customs officer – who'd already been and gone – too early at seven-thirty hours. This seemed unfair on the dock master since Tad had radioed ahead with an expected time of arrival of seven o'clock which they were never likely to make. Having failed to radio ahead with an amended ETA, Tad was now taking it out on the unfortunate dock master for an oversight of his own making. Consequently, they now had to wait several more hours until the local Customs officer was summoned a second time from Cat Island some miles away. After taking on fuel, the crew fussed over warps and fenders and kept their own counsel about Tad's behaviour.

Some of this questionable conduct could be attributed to his anxiety over the fact that this was their last landfall before Port Antonio in Jamaica. Later that night, he and Ewan wandered across the island's airstrip to the bar where, over a rum and coke, he confided his unease about the boat's level of preparedness for such a long voyage across the Pacific 'in one of the remotest corners of the world.' During this initial stage, it was the vessel's engine system that was proving unpredictable rather than its sails and rigging.

Ewan sought to reassure him that things would probably bed down and come right under the constant maintenance effort of the past week. Inwardly, though, the thought of venturing thousands of miles into this vast body of water in such a vessel – beautiful though she may appear – sent a twinge of angst through his stomach. He reassured himself with the knowledge that Jamaica and Panama were still ahead where further repairs and tweaking could be made.

At eleven-thirty next day, *Bella Mama* sailed out of Hawk's Nest on a southerly course down Exuma Sound. They passed Rum Cay and Conception Island, on their eastern flank, and Long Island, on the west. After Christopher Columbus landed on the island of San Salvador in October 1492 – his first footing on the New World -- he proceeded with six captive Indians to these islands (now called Rum Cay) which he named Santa Maria de la Concepcion, and to Long Island, which he called Fernandina. During the early settlement of Hispaniola, many Bahamian Indians were transported there as slaves by the Spanish and the islands were eventually depopulated through disease and brutality. From the mid-sixteenth century, Spain's enemies – notably the French and English – used the islands as a base from which to attack her treasure-laden galleons. And so began a history of piracy that would endure for the next two hundred years.

In the distance, they skirted the low profile of Acklin's Island and the Castle Island lighthouse at its southwest tip. After almost twenty-four hours of brisk twenty-knot wind from the southeast, they were on a course of 162 degrees towards Cuba and the Windward Passage that separated it from Haiti to the east. The mainsail was almost fully extended and well balanced by a taut staysail that gave them a steady six knots over the ground. Overnight, the wind weakened and – as if in protest – Ewan's lee-cloth bunk harness gave way and he crashed to the floor of his tiny cabin in a dazed heap where he remained in squalid discomfort. Then, to add insult to injury, his port light started leaking...copiously. Later, he grumbled to the skipper about poor workmanship.

Tad made him a platter of pancakes, maple syrup with a blob of yoghurt and rounded it off by suggesting he perform an indecent act upon himself...though not necessarily in those precise words.

'Aye, aye captain,' he laughed and disappeared into the heads.

Overnight they made good speed. But Tad was still wrestling over whether to stop in Jamaica to do repairs or sail on to Panama and do them there. Fortunately, this imposing island was on the same course as Panama and no decision needed to be taken at this juncture. The current feeling, though, was that making a stop on the north coast of Jamaica at Port Antonio would facilitate the shipment of spares from Fort Lauderdale for the ailing autopilot as well as other essential gear.

The weather conditions were glorious as they powered through the bright blue ocean on a beam reach. Overall, *Bella Mama* was sailing to perfection at around seven knots. They had covered a distance of one hundred and eighty-nine nautical miles over the past twenty-four hours. Ewan cooked a Chinese *chow fan* which went down well with the crew. As they rounded Punta de Maisi at the eastern tip of Cuba and sailed into the Windward Passage, they altered course to two-twenty-five degrees and Ewan's three-hour watch began. The captain configured a goose-wing sail plan and soon they were steaming downwind at eight-point-four knots with a ten-foot swell on their heels. Being on the helm was exhilarating and, privately, he counted his blessings for such moments. The Hylas 49 was a good sailing machine.

As they passed the rugged cliffs of Cuba, Ewan impulsively shouted an insane salute to this gutsy little nation and its indomitable leader:

'Viva Cuba! Viva Fidel!' he yelled without knowing exactly why.

His Canadian *compadres* echoed the accolade with a roar of approval. Both their countries – Britain and Canada -- had embassies in Havana across the island

and recognised the Castro regime. The US did not and maintained a rigorous embargo on all forms of contact with this forlorn little Marxist outpost. Jojo and Ewan had recently sailed to Havana as crew and were inspired by its music – particularly the *salsa* – but very depressed by its economic deprivation.

It was difficult to visit Cuba and not feel a degree of anger at Washington's bullying policies and their consequences for the local population. For make no mistake, insisted Ewan, it was the blockade on trade with its mighty neighbour that explained much of the dilapidation, poverty and faded glory afflicting this former Spanish colony. Through a sustained policy of economic strangulation over four decades, America had effectively reduced Cuba to an existence of penury and universal shortages.

Listen to the propaganda put out by Cuban exiles in south Florida, of course, and all Cuba's woes stemmed from the evils of communism and Fidel Castro. For decades, the power of the Cuban lobby – backed mainly by vestiges of the former corrupt Batista regime -- had warped American policy and painted Washington into yet another ideological corner from which it seemed unable to escape. Few Americans of his acquaintance supported this mistreatment of their tiny neighbour but seemed unable to do anything about it. Such was the power, it seemed, of minority lobbyists within America's rambling political system.

Around Cuba's eastern headland, on its southern coast, sat the US base at Guantanamo Bay, one of the great anomalies of contemporary geopolitics. Parked on the skinny rump of Castro's communist republic, this was the location to which America had shepherded international terrorist suspects, notably those associated with the Taliban in Afghanistan and El-Qaida in Iraq and the Middle East. It was also where it momentarily re-wrote the Geneva Convention's rules on the treatment and interrogation of prisoners of war. As they proceeded through the Windward Passage, *Bella Mama* was over-taken by two southbound freighters. Otherwise, no vessels were visible on any horizon.

They were, of course, conscious that their progress was closely monitored by Uncle Sam's formidable electronic surveillance machinery -- satellite and radar – but assumed an air of moral superiority. This was pretty irrational, of course, when Ewan pondered Britain's treatment of irritating Caribbean islands over the past three hundred years...

The difficulty with Europe's anti-Americanism – particularly over the latter's treatment of Cuba – was that countries like Britain, France, Holland, Spain and Portugal all had their own questionable baggage in this part of the world...to do with colonialism, economic vandalism, piracy and, lest he overlooked a significant chapter, four hundred years of trans-Atlantic slavery. They sailed on into the night reflecting upon national hypocrisy and the luxury of impotence...

Twelve

Their brilliant run south came to a halt when the wind weakened and *Bella Mama* started wallowing in a sea of uncomfortable and disjointed wave patterns. The engine had failed to start again the previous night so the skipper had definitely decided to make a stopover in Port Antonio on the northeast coast of Jamaica. This was good news as it would give them the opportunity to do some sightseeing and, hopefully, sort out some of the boat's recurring mechanical problems at the same time. As the Raytheon auto-pilot had joined its backup partner -- the Autohelm 7000 -- in ceasing to work, they were now steering the yacht in the old-fashioned way: manually. Consequently, the crew was organised into three-hour helm-watches as they motored into the night.

Next morning they woke to find themselves surrounded on all sides by multitudes of dolphins streaking in every direction through the sombre blue waters and cavorting across their bows. On the far horizon ahead, the mountainous profile of Jamaica began to appear although, as yet, there was still no sign of Port Antonio along the coastline. The charts indicated a sizeable lighthouse at its entrance which would soon hove into view. The mood on board was upbeat and helped by the presence of frolicking dolphins and bright skies. Tad produced another of his gourmet omelettes for the crew -- this time stuffed with cheese, zucchini, tomato and mushrooms – and topped it with a scoop of sour cream all of which was equally shared out on three plates. For himself, the skipper prepared an alternative version that included the remains of Ewan's chicken curry from last night's dinner. The boy had flair…if you liked a curry filling in your omelette. And there was still enough *rogan gosht*

– always better on the second day -- for the evening meal.

As they got closer, Jamaica began to look very attractive from the northern approaches with its towering mountains looming out of the blue Caribbean Sea and shrouded in cotton-wool cloud. The island seemed very luxuriant and the high-points were dotted everywhere with *bella vista* mansions set within imposing grounds. The outer reefs and coastal promontories required careful navigation as they made their way towards the palm-fringed inner harbour of Port Antonio, lining up several on-shore transit markers in the process. At the time, Nicola was on the helm while Tad decided, unannounced, to shimmy up the two mid-ship shrouds to the lower mast spreaders so as to take pictures with his new digital camera. His athleticism was impressive but Ewan wondered if this was where the skipper ought to be at such a moment.

Nicola was in no doubt. She was nervous and panicky about misreading the markers and steering their fast-moving vessel into troubled waters. She was unhappy at the skipper's lofty perch halfway up the mast instead of by her side as they entered an unfamiliar port. As a result, they motored into this splendid haven to the din of an acrimonious altercation between a helmsman on deck and a captain aloft. Since Tad had already shown himself to be a very hands-on – some might say meddlesome – skipper, the crew were generally reluctant to make decisions without his prior consent. Hence Nicola's unease.

She then threw what could only be called a red-head's tantrum, recklessly abandoning the helm and disappearing below deck in a flood of tears. Tad streaked down the shrouds like a demented monkey and took control of the wheel. Both elements of the team – helm and skipper – had hardly displayed sound judgement or professionalism on this occasion. Indeed, Nicola's outburst seemed childish and did not augur well for the more testing times that lay ahead. They would have to see, as time went by, how relations developed between this feisty, freckle-faced madam and her very controlling captain.

They made their way into the marina and docked stern-to in Mediterranean fashion, for a six-day stopover, awaiting the arrival of various spare parts being air-freighted from Fort Lauderdale. Over this period they were assigned on-board repair and cleaning duties by the ever-attentive boss. Initially, Tad rationed shore leave but gave them sufficient time to explore Port Antonio.

It turned out to be a somewhat shabby town of faded colonial architecture whose inhabitants lounged about in a soporific mood of ganja-induced lethargy and the enforced idleness of under-employment. There were, however, lively street markets selling a wide array of fresh produce and merchandise where energy levels ran a little higher.

Tad, in the meantime, befriended the marina's dock-master. John was stocky, ebony black and in his early forties. He wore thigh-tight Bermuda shorts and, like most Jamaican males, considered himself something of a stud. To prove this point, he regaled them with lurid details of his daily obligations to a middle-aged German woman who was single-handing a forty-foot sloop anchored in the bay. Each afternoon, recounted John, he would abandon his post and dinghy out to give this over-tanned *frau* from Stuttgart what he called "summa de black mahn's stuff." One wondered if she realised just how well-briefed her fellow mariners were about these extra-curricular gymnastics. All of which aroused in our captain a certain degree of interest in the sexual mores and proclivities of the natives…as they later discovered.

Next day – with John and his interpreter in tow – Tad rented a car with his owner's credit card and headed into the dramatic Blue Mountains that run along the eastern end of Jamaica. Once off the coastal strip, they wound their way along narrow sealed roads into the hills passing through sleepy villages and stopping at various wayside pubs and cafes to eat local meat patties (a sort of Jamaican Cornish Pasty) and pastries. At one of these establishments, the barmaid was a local beauty – a young mulatto woman with stunning blue eyes set within a brown Afro-Caribbean face -- who introduced them to a popular Jamaican cocktail of Stone's Ginger Wine and Appleton's over-proofed rum. They downed a few of these then headed back to the car and drove up-country into the rain and mist.

Once over the watershed, with sweeping vistas across the island's south side towards Kingston, Jamaica's capital city, they stopped to take photographs. The air was permeated by the pungent aroma of freshly-roasted coffee...and the distant chatter of English accents. They investigated and came upon an elderly white couple on their veranda plus their daughter and two grandchildren. He was seventy and originally from London having come to Jamaica some forty years earlier to work as a chartered surveyor when it was still a British colony; she was a white Jamaican of similar age. Their bungalow overlooked a hundred-acre plantation of some 100,000 coffee bushes which they were rescuing from dereliction since retiring from local government service ten years earlier.

After harvesting, the coffee beans were roasted at the plantation and then trucked down to a Kingston warehouse on the coast. Marketing of their particular brand of the much sought-after Blue Mountain Coffee was done via internet to restaurants and private clients in New York, Miami, San Francisco, Taiwan, Japan and elsewhere around the world. They employed about thirty workers as pickers -- mainly women from neighbouring villages – and also had another home in the suburbs of Kingston. The plantation, explained the couple, was their retirement job and afforded them a very full and active life and created work for the local villagers.

According to ebony John, white Jamaican families that still lived on the island were often those connected with the old plantation culture that dominated the local economy for centuries. While the ownership of these ventures had often been in the hands of absentee landlords in Britain, their management was frequently left to white plantation managers and foremen whose antecedents went back to the days before the abolition of slavery in 1833. The lady of the house, he said, was part of the old "bookie master" class that once held sway on this and neighbouring islands. From the tone of his voice, one gathered they were not the most popular survivors of the old slave culture and colonial order that once shaped the socio-economic complexion of this island.

SLAVERY

It was the Spanish and Portuguese who, in the fifteenth century, first introduced African slavery to the Caribbean. England was said to have entered the trade in 1560 when Sir John Hawkins sold a cargo of three hundred slaves captured in Sierra Leone to Spanish colonists in the Caribbean island of Hispaniola. In 1662, in order to promote the sugar cane industry in Barbados, the Royal Adventure Trading Company was chartered by Charles II and received a contract for the delivery of three thousand Negro slaves a year to the British West Indies.

This human traffic was supplied through a chain of consolidating forts and castles along the West African coast. These slave depots were legalised under the Asiento Treaty of 1713 which allowed traders to sell slaves at certain authorised ports in Spanish and British colonies. For this privilege they paid a duty of approximately $40 per slave, a quarter of which went to the Spanish and British crowns. By the middle of the eighteenth century, Jamaica's slave population alone was estimated at a quarter of a million.

The Spanish were the first Europeans to settle Jamaica in 1509 and in 1534 they moved the capital to Villa de Vega, now called Spanish Town. Initially, they forced the indigenous Arawak Indians to work as their slaves in the gold mines and plantations of neighbouring islands. By the early seventeenth century, however, nearly all the Arawaks had been wiped out through a combination of European diseases and mistreatment. Initially, imported black slaves from Africa became the alternative labour force under Spanish rule and, later, under the British who had gained control of Jamaica by 1655.

Curiously, Jamaica never achieved the same degree

of strategic importance as other Spanish Caribbean islands as a consolidation point along the trade routes between Spain and the Americas. But by 1660 the British controlled the island and it briefly degenerated into a haven for piracy and general lawlessness until the suppression of these activities by 1670. During this period, British buccaneers operating from Port Royal were able to attack Spanish vessels and outposts with relative impunity.

As the English and Spanish struggled for control of the island, many slaves formerly held by the Spanish rulers managed to escape into the mountains. Known as Maroons, they briefly developed an independent culture and lived outside British control until the 1730s on condition that they returned any runaway slaves to the plantations from which they had escaped. Although Spain was the first to bring African slaves to the island, Britain later imported an increasing number of these unfortunate souls to Jamaica in the eighteenth century to work its flourishing sugar economy.

While many slaves were sold on to other British colonies in North and South America, most were kept in Jamaica to augment the plantation labour force and transform it into what was then the world's largest sugar producer. Consequently, by the early eighteenth century Jamaica had become Britain's most lucrative territory in the New World; which perhaps explains the limited effort made by London to retain control of its thirteen American colonies after the Battle of Yorktown in 1781. In broad economic terms, Jamaica, Barbados and her other Caribbean territories were generating far greater wealth for the mother country and its investors than her struggling colonies along the eastern seaboard of North America. And at this point in history, colonialism was more about financial gain than imperial aggrandisement.

A century-and-a-half after annexing Jamaica, the passage of Britain's protracted anti-slavery movement was formalised in March 1807 with a statute decreeing that no vessel engaged in the slave trade could be cleared from any port of the British Dominions and no slave could be imported into any British colony after March 1808. Spear-headed by the English parliamentarian, William Wilberforce, the abolition movement would eventually culminate in the Emancipation Act of August 1833, which freed all slaves within the British Empire. As part of this legislation, Parliament indemnified the planters through a £20 million appropriation for the losses incurred to their slave assets by this legislation.

So engrained had this odious traffic become throughout most of the Americas – including the Caribbean – that blockade running by slave ships persisted for many more years. To support its altered moral stance, meanwhile, London established the British West Africa Squadron charged with enforcing its abolitionist laws and ensuring that no British captains traded slaves along three thousand miles of the African coast. In addition, a bounty of £60 per male, £30 per female and £10 per child was paid by the Admiralty to naval officers and other beneficiaries for every slave liberated.

Through a persistent use of naval power and diplomatic wrangling – notably with countries like the United States, France, Spain, Portugal and Brazil where slavery had yet to be comprehensively outlawed – Britain assumed a position of moral leadership that atones, to some degree, for its earlier enthusiasm for this grim trade. In his masterful work The Slave Trade, Hugh Thomas estimates that some 2.6 million of the eleven million Negroes transported to the Americas over the four-hundred-year history of transatlantic slavery were on British-flagged vessels, second only to Portugal's figure of 4.65 million (mainly to Brazil).

Initially, the eradication of slavery did not augur well for Jamaica's sugar industry which declined significantly throughout the nineteenth century, due partly to the loss of its enslaved labour force. The slave rebellion of 1831 added to the difficulties facing white plantation owners coupled with Britain's decision in 1846 to remove tariff protection for Jamaican sugar. For their part, the freed slaves became embittered by the persistent effort of the plantations to force them to continue working the estates after emancipation. This the owners were able to do through a white colonial oligarchy that controlled the local government and, through the judiciary, imposed discriminatory taxation, denied land to former slaves and allowed unfair competition from imported Indian and Chinese indentured labour as well as freed-Africans from captured slave ships.

Eventually, this cauldron of injustice erupted into the rebellion of 1865 which, although brutally suppressed by the British government, began the island's slow progress towards political autonomy. Concerned at the level of unrest throughout what had once been one of the empire's most prized assets, London imposed direct rule by transforming Jamaica into a crown colony. This arrangement survived until 1959, when full internal self-government was attained, followed three years later by total political independence from Britain within the Commonwealth with the British Monarch as Jamaica's formal head of state.

Some of these thoughts percolated through Ewan's mind as he considered the irony of this modest post-retirement enterprise in the mountains above Port Antonio and its quaint cast of characters. Although clearly unused to this sudden influx of outsiders, they were extremely welcoming and – after a tour of the facilities—invited them to a pot of their home-grown coffee along with several slices of Jamaica currant bun and coffee honey, a local delicacy.

Their visit to a Blue Mountain coffee plantation had been a somewhat unexpected bonus and a poignant reminder of the harsh plantation culture that had once dominated this island economy. Today, Jamaica had a more democratic agricultural sector than in colonial times, he thought. It also benefited appreciably from international tourism earnings. But the brutalising of its people over the centuries had left a legacy of crime and lawlessness which successive local and overseas governments continue to battle.

Thirteen

Ebony John told Tad that Kerry-Anne – the chocolate maiden with the blue eyes in the village bar down the hill – would 'probably like to have her bottom smacked by a white man…and a few other things besides'. This was just what Tad wanted to hear. He engaged second gear and sped down the winding Blue Mountains road like a tomcat on heat until they reached the Appleton's Rum sign at the side of the road. They parked the rental on the dirt sidewalk, sauntered into the tiny tavern, resumed their seats at the bar and…awaited Kerry-Anne's grand entry. The whole process had about it the prelude to a rather ponderous pornographic movie.

The blue-eyed goddess emerged from backstage and poured another round of rum-and-ginger fireballs. They downed them with manly aplomb and asked for the same again. Faced with the prospect of two white men, Kerry-Anne was spoilt for choice. Being of mixed race, she enjoyed a higher standing in the pantheon of Caribbean womanhood than her blacker sisters. With tonight's line-up, explained ebony John, this ruled him out of play. He was very matter-of-fact about such sensitive racial issues and was obviously accustomed to play pimp to transiting white *matelots*. After feasting his eyes on her voluptuous form, Ewan bowed out and left the field to Tad who was young, lean and bursting with testosterone.

Next day -- after a two-hour bus ride from her village in the Blue Mountains -- Kerry-Anne arrived at the marina in Port Antonio and boarded *Bella Mama* to have her bottom smacked by a white man 'and a few other things besides.' These included becoming an honorary crew member and taking up residence in the captain's state room until they departed a few days later. She was young and flirtatious and her lilting Jamaican brogue brought a breath of Caribbean innocence to their tight little yachtie world.

But Tad's dalliance had two dangerous by-products: it extended *Bella Mama's* stopover in Jamaica by several days thus incurring her distant owners extra expense in marina costs and salaries -- a risky ploy, warned Ewan; and – more dangerous still – it conjured up that lethal green-eyed monster called female jealousy in the resident red-head. Nicola was neither impressed by Kerry-Anne's cheeky Jamaican charm nor her onboard presence.

Next day, while the captain and his girl explored each other's bodies in the privacy of his – or more precisely the owners' – spacious state room, the rest of the crew, all three of them, went for a drive in the rental.

'What else are we supposed to do?' protested an indignant Nicola.

Consequently, not much progress was made readying *Bella Mama* for the next leg of her five-hundred-and-forty-seven-mile passage from Jamaica to Panama. They drove out of Port Antonio and followed the A4 coast road east towards Northeast Point. The scenery was a feast of palm-fringed sandy coves and calm translucent creeks. Imposing residential properties looked down on the coast and out over the Caribbean Sea to the north.

They stopped for a swim and took lunch in a beach café before driving back to Port Antonio in the afternoon to explore the bustling weekend markets. Ewan struck up a conversation with two rather distinguished looking Jamaican gentlemen in Harris Tweed jackets. One was a retired postman from Croydon; the other a retired bus driver from Manchester. After almost forty years as black migrants in Britain, they had returned to their homeland for a more comfortable way of life. They were part of a large population of returning Jamaicans whose pensions – underpinned by a strong British pound – gave them a considerably higher standard of living in the Caribbean than the one they had enjoyed back in Mother England.

'But things don't work so good here,' they admitted, 'and de roads is shit. But yea mahn, we's retired.'

They shared a Red Stripe and drank to retirement…man's perfect state, agreed the unlikely trio.

Next day, another incident added to Nicola's mood of discontent. In addition to recurring bouts of seasickness, menstrual headaches, stomach upsets and skin rashes, their vexed colleague accidentally splashed teak stain into her eyes and face while re-arranging the contents of the stern lockers. Since nobody was quite sure how dangerous this substance might be to her eyesight and complexion, a great deal of water was poured over Nicola's face and into her tearful eyes. She was then whisked off to a nearby German doctor who prescribed a mild anti-biotic and said no damage appeared to have been done by this unfortunate incident. But Nicola and Chuck used it as a pretext for attacking Tad's captaincy. They also complained that their contribution to the efficient operation of the boat was not being sufficiently recognised.

Tad reacted to this sudden deterioration in onboard respect for his authority by threatening a crew change when they reached Panama, their next port of call. In a discreet aside, however, he assured Ewan he would be retained and only the couple would go. This induced in Ewan a mild sense of unease as to the likelihood of ever completing this trans - Pacific adventure. All three of these individuals – the skipper and his two Vancouver crew members – had been friends prior to this trip. He wondered if, perhaps, Nicola once had a crush on Tad and that his fling with this Caribbean beauty was something she'd not bargained for. Jealousy was an unpredictable passion. Whatever the history, Nicola now dragooned her compliant husband into her dissenting camp from where he obediently echoed her displeasure. While the captain sowed his wild oats, respect for his conduct appeared to be waning.

Nicola's visit to the doctor delayed their departure from Port Antonio by another day. When eventually they did cast off and departed from the picturesque little bay, it was with a certain sense of relief on the part of Ewan. Kerry-Anne waved a tearful farewell from the marina jetty. There had been solemn commitments by her and her roving paramour to reunite after the passage to New Zealand was completed. The crew, meanwhile, returned to their exacting shipboard duties and discipline. It had not always been comfortable playing gooseberry to Tad's onboard carousing. A 49-foot yacht could be a surprisingly small place when so much carnal energy was being expended.

The earlier sense of adventure and anticipation which the odyssey had engendered now began to return as they motored along Jamaica's northeast coast and rounded Morant Point Lighthouse. There was virtually no wind for the next twenty-four hours as *Bella Mama* cruised south towards Panama, about five hundred and fifty nautical miles away. They had approximately four days' fuel to cover a five-day passage. So wind, or its absence, assumed some importance in the scheme of things. But Tad assured them that onshore convections could be expected as they approached the Columbian coast which would bring wind. In the meantime, the vessel lurched uncomfortably from side to side in a gentle swell, her well-rounded hull not making for a particularly smooth ride in such conditions.

They proceeded into the night in jovial mood. The Yanmar sounded uncharacteristically healthy and – notwithstanding some critical observations about unreliable Japanese marine engines -- drove them through the water at a comfortable five to six knots. Overhead, an inky sky studded with stars and planets, provided a magnificent canopy. Ewan's mind wandered and pondered the complex matter of a former wife, a new partner and difficulties relating to the prostate gland...then returned to the more mundane matter of staying on course. It was March the twenty-eighth and good to be sailing again.

Next morning – after a hearty breakfast – Tad slung a line and spinner off the stern and within ten minutes was fighting a very determined dolphin fish. But he failed to net the creature and their hopes for a fresh fish supper were lost to the ocean depths. Instead, Ewan reworked the remains of yesterday's *chilli con carne* which, along with a bed of rice and a blob of sour cream, provided the crew with a popular bedtime feast. They'd been motoring for over twenty-four hours and now had to switch to the other ninety-gallon fuel tank which gave them another forty-five hours of engine time.

His next watch was from midnight to three o'clock. As night sailing goes, the conditions could not have been more agreeable. He prayed nothing would happen between now and their departure from Panama to abort plans for the forthcoming trans-Pacific passage. This really was a voyage he wanted to make. All being well, there would be countless night watches like this under blue-black, starry skies as they slowly made their way across the equator and into that mighty ocean. Tad surfaced from below deck and prepared to take his watch from three until six o'clock. It was Good Friday and over two thousand years since Christ was crucified. A mind adrift on such a vast stage could experience random and uncoordinated thoughts, some driven by lifelong anxieties and others by the sheer splendour of a nocturnal setting.

As the night sky gave way to dawn, Tad unleashed the spinnaker which filled comfortably in the light early-morning airs and pushed *Bella Mama* on its southerly course at a steady six knots. After coffee, Ewan switched on his portable radio and picked up various Colombian stations and listened to the news in Spanish. Easter – *Semana Santa* – was an important religious festival in the Hispanic world and a time for Christian homilies. Another suicide bomb had gone off in Israel killing twenty, reported the station. And closer to home in Cartagena – where convoys of Spanish treasure galleons once formed -- a landslide had killed six souls including a fireman.

Much of the morning was spent hoisting the skipper up the mast for more aerial photography; and reconfiguring as well as balancing the spinnaker and mainsail. Tad was exceedingly fussy about avoiding rope and sail chaffing of any kind and considerable effort was made to prevent such wear and tear. On a long voyage, micro-management of this kind was important. Ewan was learning much from this excellent young mariner where sailboat operations were concerned. His attention to detail was exhausting.

His man-management skills – or perhaps his woman-management skills -- were less impressive. On a small vessel like this, it was difficult to know which of these qualities was more important: leadership or seamanship. Both would be ideal. But boats and their captains were seldom that obliging.

During his years of apprenticeship, Tad had frequently succumbed to the despotic rule of skippers –

some more judicious than others – because that appeared to be what was expected of crew. In his desire to please and avoid confrontation, it had never occurred to him to challenge orders or question decisions. In his mind's eye, he was building a career for himself as a skilled, professional yacht sailor wherein good seamanship automatically begat good leadership. Obeying orders was the name of the game; turning the cockpit into a parliamentary democracy was not.

Despite warning hints from Ewan, it hadn't occurred to Tad that costly delays in Port Antonio spent philandering with this Jamaican bar girl – while in no way undermining his reputation as the skilled operator of a sailing yacht – was eroding respect for his integrity as a leader. Ironically, Tad assumed such extra-curricular activity was actually enhancing his image as the glamorous, swashbuckling macho captain he so desperately wanted to be and not the opposite.

Fourteen

They encountered very little shipping – large or small – between Jamaica and Panama. But soon there were indications of landfall as ships began to converge on all sides. If nothing else, this reassured them that *Bella Mama*'s navigation aids were performing as required and keeping them on the right course. There was also a certain comfort – a human comfort -- in the presence of other vessels after the solitude of recent days.

Another barometer for the lonely *matelot* was the radio. Even a humble, twenty-dollar Radio Shack portable brought a cacophony of languages, music and voices over the air waves as they sailed within range of nearby transmitters. At four o'clock, under a star-studded sky, Ewan flicked a switch and out of nowhere came the warm, reassuring sounds of human voices reaching out across the enormousness of sea and sky. As they approached the Republic of Panama – which until 1903 had been part of neighbouring Colombia -- the lisping staccato of Latin American Spanish wafted across the ether and brought tears to his eyes.

He couldn't fully explain this emotion…but whenever certain languages were spoken, sung or even shouted he sometimes felt a deep sense of well-being tinged with profound nostalgia. Spanish was one of those emotive triggers. Perhaps it had something to do with a couple of chilly winters spent in Barcelona teaching English and French at the Berlitz School in the early 1960s. Shortly after arriving in this elegant Catalan metropolis, he met a man from Kent called Ross who had already spent many years in Franco's Spain and spoke the language like a native. Ross became a good friend and his mentor on most things to do with Spain.

His anecdotes and adventures about a land still relatively unknown to the rest of Europe in the early sixties enriched Ewan's youthful soul and filled him with an enthusiasm for its welcoming culture and lifestyle. Ross was a dedicated expatriate who had embraced Spain -- regardless of its fascist government and economic backwardness – and, in the process, rejected most things to do with Britain. He was also an alcoholic, a Roman Catholic and decidedly Anglo-Irish in ethnicity and outlook. All of which had, in various ways, contributed to an apparent hostility to his native land.

With its abundant supply of cheap wines and spirits, Spain in those days was a drinker's paradise. General Franco's pro-Vatican foreign policy also sat comfortably with an English catholic like Ross accustomed to life on the edge of the great Christian divide. Ross had enough Irish blood in his veins to prejudice him very much in Dublin's favour over the then unresolved problems of Northern Ireland. All of which created a hugely complex but likeable character fractured by a host of conflicting opinions and loyalties. And nothing gave Ross more pleasure than winding up and teasing a gullible youth about his 'stuffy Presbyterian attitudes.' These exchanges, one should add, took place in a variety of sedate Barcelona bars over many cups of café-cognac and filter-tipped Ducados; a perfect setting for the armchair politician and gifted raconteur.

Whatever it was that induced this nostalgia – memories of a departed friend, the Spanish language or a youthful golden era -- the sounds emanating from Radio de Colombia that night made a welcome change from the calypso babble of the Anglo-Caribbean stations usually choking the airwaves in these waters.

On night passages, his mind often drifted aimlessly from one unrelated thought to the next triggered by evocative prompts like sound, smell, taste or random imagination. Even three hundred miles offshore, Colombia sounded infinitely more sophisticated than Jamaica's banana boat culture with its ganja-doped Rastafarians and Kingston gangsters. As the skies lightened on the port bow and the first signs of another day began to dawn, the exciting prospect of navigating the Panama Canal now dominated his thoughts. Anticipation of great things to come was so important in life. It was time for morning coffee.

Nicola emerged early to inform them that Chuck had contracted her recent bout of flu and was not in best shape. He would stay below deck and she would undertake his helm duties. One wondered what additional ailments might afflict the Vancouver couple on the much longer passage from Panama to Tahiti. After mumbled commiserations, the skipper decided to have another shot at deep-sea fishing…this time with more success. The long line tightened and whipped wildly as a four-foot barracuda took the bait and sounded for deeper water. But its battle for survival -- lasting almost fifteen minutes – was in vain as Tad and crew gradually shortened its scope and brought it to the surface. From the transom platform, Tad's skills with the gaffe hook improved as he coaxed their silvery catch into the net and onto the deck. Its red gills dilated, its tale threshed and – after a few blows to the head with a hefty winch handle – it was gutted and sent to the galley for rendering. They ate fish for the next few days and froze the rest. *Bella Mama*'s crew enjoyed a quiet sense of satisfaction, confident in the knowledge that, even if the Yanmar and wind failed, they could still survive on a diet of *fruits de mer* and rainwater.

But these distractions came at a price. They had

wandered off course. The prevailing winds and current had dragged them too far west of Puerto Cristobal y Colon, the principal Atlantic gateway to the Panama Canal for which they were headed. As the wind increased, they snuffed the spinnaker, unfurled the genoa and surged ahead at seven knots on a beam reach in order to regain easterly longitude. Tad put out a short-wave radio call to Brian and Lorraine, an Australian couple circumnavigating the globe in a home-made catamaran that they had met earlier in Port Antonio. They reported calm seas and a lack of wind and appeared to have fallen well behind them to the west.

'See you in Panama squire,' ended Brian. 'Don't drink all the grog.'

Before retirement, Brian had been a senior officer in the Royal Australian Air Force at the ministry of defence in Canberra. He'd also spent many years based at the British missile range in Woomera working on the short-lived Black Knight and Blue Streak programmes, Britain's last gasp at developing an independent rocket and space capability. After quitting the air force, Brian built his own catamaran *Mara* – named after an Aboriginal tribe -- and had spent the past eight years with his wife circumnavigating the world. After the Panama Canal, they were on their last leg across the Pacific back to Sydney.

Tedium set in and Ewan began to contemplate, not for the first time, the pros and cons of long blue-water passages such as the one he was currently undertaking. He also reminded himself that this was a delivery operation and they were all being paid. The mood and atmosphere on such trips was bound to be less casual than mere sailing for pleasure. Two months at sea aboard a small vessel was a long voyage involving considerable discipline and routine. These qualities they had. One also had to remember this was not their yacht and that certain professional standards had to be observed in order to comply with insurance requirements and the expectations of their American owners.

It had also become pretty clear that *Bella Mama* was not a trouble-free vessel. The forward head blocked and the generator motor continued to give problems which affected the refrigeration and other power-dependent systems. Add to this some questionable wiring and a couple of delinquent autopilots and the prospect of crossing the Pacific Ocean in such a vessel began to create a sense of unease. Tad said she was a ten-year-old yacht which had not always been well cared for by previous owners and operators. On that score, he was certainly right.

Since leaving Florida three weeks ago their progress had been interrupted by a series of technical breakdowns. This naturally prompted the crew to ask why these shortcomings were not detected when the boat was being readied for this long voyage at Summerfield's. Too much effort, it would seem, had gone into the topside overhaul of sails and rigging and not enough into below-deck engine and electronic systems. All this mutinous chatter, of course, was out of Tad's ear-shot.

Ewan, meanwhile, distracted himself from such matters by taking on an extra share of galley duties. This was partly because Chuck and Nicola's various ailments, interspersed with occasional bouts of seasickness, effectively excused them galley duties. Nicola's emphasis on vegetarian meals and organic food also resulted in some fairly un-appetising fare, particularly when compared to Tad's splendid *cordon bleu* efforts. But the skipper had weightier matters on his mind and did not expect to be their galley slave. So

Ewan willingly volunteered for extra cooking duties if only to customise meals more to his own tastes. Selfish, he conceded, but eating crap food – no matter how healthy – had never been his idea of sailing pleasure…least of all for weeks on end.

Another important by-product of these extra cooking duties was finding out where all the food supplies were located. Prior to leaving Fort Lauderdale, Chuck and Nicola had been assigned the task – under the skipper's watchful eye -- of carefully wrapping and stowing their victuals. *Bella Mama* was not only well endowed with lockers but had countless spaces under the saloon and cabin decks between the hull ribs where foodstuffs could be stored. As part of the process, all fresh fruit and vegetables, for example, had been carefully wrapped in newspaper and then squirreled away under foot. Wrapping in paper, explained Tad, was the best way to extend the life of fresh greens and fruit at sea. More perishable items like meats, butter and milk had been consigned to the refrigerator or the capacious freezer. Biscuits, cereals, pulsars and other dry goods could be found just about anywhere.

Initially, this presented no difficulty because Nicola and Chuck were on hand to indicate where the various items could be found, assuming they remembered. Once they disappeared into their crowded v-berth up front, however, finding where ingredients were located became even more difficult than cobbling them into a meal.

This hurdle was eventually overcome by producing a food inventory storage plan, but not before a heated altercation between skipper and crew as to its relevance. Having not been part of the original storage exercise, Ewan was now gradually able to build a picture in his mind of where to find food and beverage items at any time of day and night. Boats at sea, he insisted, were twenty-four hour operations just like their crews and easy access to supplies was essential.

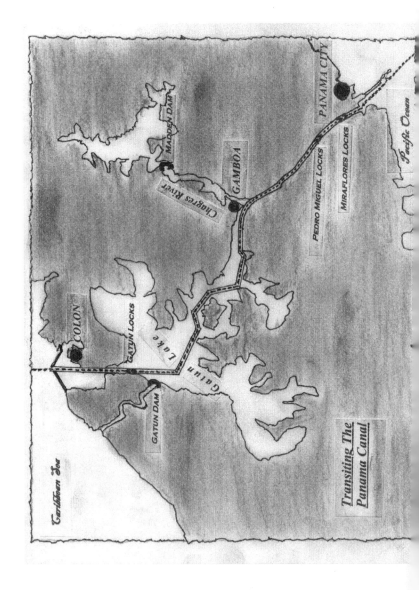

Transiting The
Panama Canal

102

Fifteen

Any vessel powered by an engine prone to unpredictable bouts of failure was not the sort of customer that organisations like the Panama Canal Authority sought to attract. In this respect, the PCA was probably no different to other great waterways like the Suez Canal or the Saint Lawrence Seaway; and the reasons were not hard to fathom. A vessel that broke down in such confined waters had the potential to block the efficient flow of traffic in much the same way as an overturned lorry on a British motorway. Ships, with their huge tonnage and valuable cargoes, moved around the oceans of the world adhering to tight schedules and anything man-made that impeded such efficiency was, as it were, *persona non grata*. Not surprisingly, therefore, hefty fines could be imposed by PCA lock-keepers on delinquent craft – big or small – that broke this golden rule.

As *Bella Mama* sailed towards the Panama Canal's busy anchorages and approaches, therefore, its crew and captain were gripped by a sense of foreboding. For as far as the eye could see there were ships either at anchor or entering and departing this remarkable umbilicus connecting the Atlantic and Pacific oceans. After the relative tranquillity of their passage from Jamaica, the shock of seeing so many large ocean vessels gathered in one place filled them with a sense of awe and wonderment. At forty-nine feet, their diminutive size and insignificance seemed palpable. The mere idea of engine failure in such a place was too awful to contemplate. So they sailed into Puerto Cristobal y Colon muttering silent prayers to all known deities of the deep.

After long hours under sail, it was now time to reef

the mainsail, furl the genoa…and fire up the engine. This was not the sort of place where a captain insisted on entering port under canvas. Such refinements were for weekend purists on the Solent or Long Island Sound, declared Tad, not for those about to tackle the Panama Canal. They all agreed. Once again, he pressed the starter button and – true to form – the Yanmar failed to respond. Sweating profusely, the skipper tore open the engine hatch and started his solitary task of trouble-shooting while *Bella Mama* drifted aimlessly in a light breeze. Some time later, he emerged to inform his crew that the deep-cycle starter battery was, after all, the root cause of the problem. A set of hastily-rigged jump leads was used to connect the other house batteries to the starter motor and – hey presto -- the Yanmar burst into life at first attempt. Hopefully, this had put an end to their engine problems.

They motored towards the outer shoreline of Cristobal y Colon and anchored at *Area F*, designated for small craft, and then dinghied into the Panama Canal Yacht Club…which turned out to be not quite as grand or salubrious as it sounded. But it did have laundry, Internet and shower facilities and a somewhat sad little bar offering draft beer at a dollar a litre.

The onshore neighbourhood – Colon – was home to a giant duty-free distribution hub of warehouses, factories and stores primarily geared to serving the wholesale consumer needs of the Latin American markets. Located at the mouth of one of the world's busiest waterways, this *entrepot* bazaar was one of several benefits Panama derived from its canal. Similarly, Panama City at the Pacific Ocean end of the canal had become a significant offshore financial centre where most of the big global institutions like HSBC, Citibank, Barclay's and UBS – to name just a few of those represented -- were prominently represented on its emerging skyline.

Unfortunately, Colon was also a hangout for local *desperados* and *contrabandistas* who make it pretty dangerous for visiting yachties to venture too far afield. In a useful little booklet on transiting the Panama Canal in a small vessel, author David Wilson notes that "anywhere outside the gates of the Panama Canal Yacht Club can be very dangerous. Thieves and pickpockets are a big problem...and it is not safe to walk around Colon anywhere or anytime." Hold-ups, he added, sometimes even occurred in the yacht club. As if to emphasise this point, the local police ride motorbikes in pairs and pack pistols on both hips, flak jackets and Uzi submachine guns across their chests. Ewan sipped *cuba libres* at the bar...then sent emails, made phone calls and did his laundry. As the first landfall in Latin America, Colon was something of a disappointment, but fellow sailors fresh from traversing the canal assured him of better things ahead.

Tad, meanwhile, made contact with their shipping agent -- a certain Tania McPherson – in order to clear *Bella Mama* and her crew through customs and immigration. All vessels were required by the PCA to have a local shipping agent to liaise with government and Panama Canal officialdom. Some of these agents specialised in handling recreational sail and power yachts and, as local residents, were a useful source of information on where to acquire various goods and services and how to deal with unforeseen complications. Most of Panama's agents concentrated on the relentless stream of freighters, tankers, bulk carriers, LNG carriers, container ships, warships and cruise liners that passed through the canal by day and night. Recreational sailboats such as *Bella Mama* were a small and no doubt irritating part of the total picture.

Tad returned with the news that their transit slot

through the canal would not be for another three days. Like the giant vessels at anchor in the deeper offshore waters, they had to wait their turn. In the shallower waters of *Area F*, a number of other sailboats laid at anchor. These were either in the same hold pattern as them or had completed their passage and were preparing for the next leg of their voyage into the Caribbean. This was useful since it gave them time to purchase a set of twelve used rubber tyres from one of these departing yachts – at three dollars per tyre – to meet PCA requirements. This was because small vessels were rafted into nests of three when proceeding through each of the six locks along the Canal and had to be amply cushioned on all sides. In such cases, the largest craft was usually positioned in the middle with the two smaller vessels flanked on either side.

With three days to kill, the crew and captain had ample time to generate *angst* and nervous tension in equal measure for the upcoming adventure. When their slot eventually materialised, therefore, they were up on deck at four-thirty in time to greet their pilot – Antonio – and his apprentice Felipe McQueen when they arrived by dinghy at five o'clock. After an introductory coffee, Antonio disappeared below deck to conclude his night's sleep while Felipe – a genial Jamaican Panamanian – took over for the rest of the day. After instructions about how things operated and what was expected of transiting vessels and their crews, they cast off their mooring buoy and motored into the main channel with lines, fenders and twelve rubber tyres all at the ready.

It was still dark as they eased into the first of three enormous up-locks and drifted towards the towering stern of a giant Swedish vehicle-carrier already in place. The ship's aft transom was like a wall and they muttered another prayer that its captain would keep his engine in neutral and the giant propellers inert. They rafted up on the port side of a three-yacht nest with a sixty-foot Swan from Australia at the centre and an American ketch called *Kela* on the starboard position. The Aussie skipper and his wife and kids were friendly and cooperative; the American up-tight and defensive. Advice emanated from all quarters. Ewan was the designated line handler on the stern port side. The tension rose. Tad attempted to project an air of casual confidence but the perspiration running down his naked back told another story. The whole setting was one of over-whelming size. Felipe -- a cool black dude of gangly proportions and impeccable dentures – was the perfect antidote to *Bella Mama's* over-stressed whities.

One of four monkey-fist lines came hurtling from high up on the lock side. Ewan attached his warp and watched it being hauled back up and walked to the optimum bollard by the tiny, distant figure of a lock operator. The same occurred on the nest's three other corners. In this way, they were held tightly in a bind until water flowed into the lock from below surface and their little threesome – not to mention the lofty Swedish freighter ahead – rose upwards as they gathered in the slackening lines with varying degrees of efficiency.

Then shrieks of alarm from *Kela*'s skipper echoed around the lock as the nest veered towards the opposite wall and his elegant ketch came within a whisker of being smashed to smithereens. This was followed by a tirade of abuse directed at Tad for not better managing his forward portside deck hands -- Chuck and Nicola -- whom he accused of not taking in the slack fast enough to keep the nest safely at the lock's centre. Tad deflected these curses onto his compatriots while the old fart up front maintained diplomatic silence.

Things calmed down and they worked their way efficiently in and out of two more lock chambers and then sailed into Lake Gatun. This initial three-stage flight of locks effectively lifted *Bella Mama* twenty-six meters from the sea-level of the Atlantic Ocean into the freshwater Lake Gatun. At the other end of the lake were three more down-locks – the Pedro Miguel and the two-step Miraflores Locks – which would eventually lower them back to sea level and into the Pacific Ocean. Before that, however, each vessel weaved its way through the lake with its jungle-clad islands and meandering channels – some of the back channels being only accessible to smaller craft -- and enjoyed the unspoilt beauty of this Smithsonian nature reserve and its discreet lodges and wildlife lookouts. Their passage across Lake Gatun and the main channel that cuts through the surrounding hills was an unexpected bonus. The spectacle of giant vessels operating within the tight confines of this beautiful setting was especially thrilling for the boat enthusiast.

As *Bella Mama* approached the three down-locks at Miraflores, Antonio – their senior pilot and advisor – told Tad to dock at a nearby PCA facility to await their turn to enter the first step of the flight, the Pedro Miguel Lock. Once tied up, they waited their turn and enjoyed a sandwich lunch while Felipe and Antonio disappeared into the nearby PCA employee canteen. The mood on board was one of quiet confidence as *Bella Mama*'s crew sunbathed in the cockpit and glimpsed the distant horizons of the Pacific Ocean through surrounding hills. Two hours later, the two Panamanian pilots returned and instructed Tad to start the engine, cast off and prepare to enter the beckoning lock and re-form the nest with *Kela* and the Aussie Swan.

Sixteen

Once again, Murphy's Law intervened and the Yanmar failed to start. Tad kept his finger on the button but the starter found no favour with its temperamental engine. One by one the down-lock slots were missed as the skipper and team – including Aussie Brian who was keen to acquire canal experience before navigating his catamaran in a few days' time – attacked the maverick motor. Brian planned to undertake three such dummy runs before bringing his own sexy yellow vessel through the canal and was, in Ewan's view, being very prudent. There had been similar plans for *Bella Mama*, but Tad's prolonged absences at Colon left them instead in limbo. Nicola was convinced he had taken a fancy to their agent which, if true, further complicated matters. The lady in question was American, spoke fluent Spanish, lived locally and was a single-parent mother.

'Perfect game for our horny *capitano*,' scoffed Nicola.

As Tad and crew were unable to fire up the engine (despite the addition of a new battery in Colon), a PCA launch was summoned to tow *Bella Mama* some fifteen miles back along the canal to Gamboa, a mid-canal turning basin. This was the nearest emergency anchorage and, if nothing else, afforded another view of the Culebra Cut and surrounding hills. The tow had taken about an hour-and-a-half to complete by the time they eventually dropped anchor after dark.

Gamboa turned out to be a small town on the south side of the canal at the confluence with the Rio Chagres. Here they discovered that most of the canal's tugs and launches were powered by Yanmar diesel engines and promptly recruited the freelance services of the first available PCA mechanic. Domingo spoke very little English so Ewan's role as interpreter proved useful. What's the Spanish for a fuel injector? he wondered. Meanwhile, the handling agent was informed of their plight by mobile and predicted onerous charges and penalties.

At present, it was hard to feel sympathy for a fussy skipper like Tad who had undertaken a Panama Canal transit with what had become such an unreliable engine. To break down midway through the Panama Canal was the ultimate embarrassment, jibed Nicola. It was noteworthy, however, that their predicament was shared on an even grander scale by two freighters that had recently collided near Gamboa due to a steering malfunction on the larger of the two. Upon impact, the smaller vessel had sunk nose down and, three weeks later, was still awaiting the arrival of welding crews from its overseas headquarters. Fortunately for the smooth running of the Panama Canal, this incident occurred off-piste in the anchorage basin and was not obstructing traffic. Things could have been worse, chimed Nicola sarcastically.

Ewan felt a twinge of sympathy for *Bella Mama*'s distant owners. Their vessel was now anchored in the delinquents' corner with the other bad boys. Domingo, Aussie Brian and Tad toiled into the night trying to discover what ailed their troubled Yanmar. The engine started briefly – their hearts soared -- and then spluttered into eerie silence. There was water in one of the cylinders, declared Brian. Ewan struggled to translate words like hydraulic decompression into understandable Spanish. Both had Latin or Greek roots so this wasn't as difficult as it seemed.

During much-needed coffee breaks, he marvelled at the number and size of vessels constantly passing as they lay at anchor like a wounded sea-gull. As *Bella Mama* was no longer positioned near any of the giant locks, the only sound as these behemoths steamed by was the deep throb of their mighty engines. The Panama Canal's traffic management system operated like a well-lubricated machine as they slid between the surrounding hills over the continental divide towards the Pacific or Atlantic oceans. The southbound schedule for the day showed about one vessel processed every half hour; a similar number passed the other way. The northbound tanker *Panam Atlantico* steamed by...four hundred and forty feet long and registered in the Bahamas. Compared to the *Sea-Land Mercury* – a fully-laden container ship of nine-hundred and fifty-eight feet – she was of modest dimensions. The *Tarago,* a seven-hundred-and-ninety-foot Norwegian roll-on/roll-off vessel, packed with motor vehicles, followed half an hour later. Next came the gleaming structure of a six hundred-and-ten-foot passenger ship called the *Regal Empress* which was also on the Bahamian register. Then the *Silver Knight,* a four-hundred-and-eighty-foot refrigerated cargo vessel from Cyprus. And so it continued around the clock.

'This is a critical artery of world trade,' pronounced Nicola with great solemnity as she eyed a passing Swedish auto carrier, 'and here's *Bella Mama* about to screw up the whole fucking process. Just think: vehicle deliveries could be slowed down and thousands of Japanese car workers thrown out of work. And what's our skipper doing -- sniffing ass in Panama City. What a scenario. It's disgusting.'

As Thadeus had just left the boat, they all enjoyed a hearty laugh at his expense. He'd gone ashore on Domingo's launch to make calls and do 'God knows what else,' shouted the flamboyant red head.

He returned next morning and the three-man team of mechanics resumed their quest for what ailed *Bella Mama*'s temperamental motor. Eventually, raw water was expelled from her cylinders, fuel made combustible and the engine burst into life and purred contentedly. Tad said they could go ashore because he had to report the good news to the agent and owners. So they piled into the dinghy and motored a short way up the Rio Chagres to a luxurious riverside hotel set in well-tended, sub-tropical gardens. Here they gazed at crocodiles, took a shower and sipped cold beer on the terrace. At which point Chuck and Nicola, somewhat dramatically and out of the blue, confided in Ewan that they had lost faith in the captain's judgment and might quit the boat at Balboa.

This was something of a shock for Ewan and raised doubts about his further involvement in the upcoming trans-Pacific passage. If they did jump ship then he had to decide on what basis, if any, he was prepared to continue. He checked his emails, made a few family calls to the UK and, later, joined the couple for a pleasant dinner in the hotel restaurant.

TWO DAYS later a portly, middle-aged American – the Panama Canal Authority's chief transit engineer – came aboard to inspect the repair work and see if *Bella Mama* was in a fit state to continue. As part of this sign-off procedure, he now required the captain to start and shut down the engine at least twelve times to determine its reliability. But he was a sympathetic sort and, rather than insisting on this tedious demonstration, accepted Tad's assurances that things were fixed.

'You fellahs know the consequences if you break down a second time?' he warned. 'But if you say it's okay then I'll accept you don't want to incur any more costs and that you can make it to Balboa.'

Balboa was at the Pacific end of the canal a few miles away and would take them outside the canal authority's jurisdiction and its costly operating environment.

'Since Uncle Sam relinquished ownership of the canal in 1999,' he explained with a mischievous grin and raised eyebrows, 'we're run much more like a business.' *Bella Mama*'s skipper paled as he was reminded of the unnecessary fines and tow charges his captaincy had already incurred in negotiating the Panama Canal. All this would have to be explained to his masters in Illinois. Tolls and fines had risen appreciably since the handover of canal ownership from the Americans to the Panamanians.

Next day agent Tania advised Tad that they had a down-lock allocation in a few hours' time and should motor back to the point where they'd broken down a few days earlier. At nine o'clock the two PCA pilots boarded *Bella Mama* along with a local line handler called Eduardo Robinson to replace the Australian. Brian was returning to his catamaran and wife in Colon in readiness for their own passage through the canal in a few days. And since his catamaran had two engines – one in each hull – he teased the crew about how his vessel had a fifty percent better prospect of making it to the Pacific Ocean than *Bella Mama.*

They motored back along the canal towards the descending flight of locks which, engine permitting, would lower them into the Pacific Ocean. The first was the Pedro Miguel Locks which, like the ascending Gatun Locks from the Atlantic, comprised two giant chambers at the same level with a centre wall and Control House from which lock activities were managed. The lock chambers were 33.5 metres wide, 305 metres long and twenty-six metres deep. Although vessels used their own propulsion for the greater part of the Panama Canal transit, they were assisted, when passing through the locks, by small electric locomotives which employed cables to align and tow the ships. Working in pairs, these "donkeys" moved on rails and kept the vessels in position within the lock chamber. Depending on size, a vessel could require the help of anything from four to eight of these locomotives to complete the task.

Small yachts did not, of course, require such assistance and made their way in and out of the locks under their own steam. As they were the only small vessel involved on this occasion, they were ordered to position *Bella Mama* in front of a refrigeration freighter hailing from Limassol which had already parked up ahead in the lock chamber. They motored past and connected the lines from their four corners to the lock handlers on shore. The Yanmar purred contentedly, showing no sign of overheating or post-traumatic stress. Was this solitary position up front assigned to *Bella Mama* because she was now notoriously branded as a canal outcast? they wondered. Felipe, whose presence had a remarkably calming effect on proceedings, assured Tad and company with a mischievous wink that 'it ain't necessarily so.' Needless to say, he was not believed.

This time, Tad kept the engine running during their passage down all three locks and again begged the help of all known deities in this their final effort to reach the Pacific Ocean. Eventually, his prayers answered, *Bella Mama* motored firstly out of Pedro Miguel Locks and then through the two-step Miraflores Locks without a moment's hesitation.

Despite all the difficulties, navigating the Panama Canal had been an immensely inspiring experience and lived up to their expectations in every possible way. For anyone who loved ships – both aesthetically and operationally – this was one of the world's great pulses of maritime trade and undoubtedly a lifetime's must-do for any blue water sailor, said Ewan. To observe these massive sea-going machines passing along the fifty-mile umbilicus between the Atlantic and the Pacific was uplifting stuff in more ways than one.

At noon, they exited the final down-lock, sailed under the Bridge of the Americas into the Pacific Ocean and anchored off the Balboa Yacht Club. Ewan rowed ashore in the dinghy and treated himself to the first of several Balboas – the local lager – and admired the voluptuous local ladies and their debonair Panamanian boyfriends perched along the club's bar.

He was reminded of Pop's childhood tales and tiny sepia photographs of the Panama Canal from days as a young Marconi radio officer on a British freighter in the early 1930s...and drank a private toast to his memory. Then he tried to imagine those intrepid Spanish explorers like Balboa and Pizarro coming over this same isthmus five hundred years ago...sensing a more tranquil and pacific world ahead. Somewhat selfishly, Ewan hoped this promise might also hold true for the next leg of their voyage to the Galapagos...if there was to be one.

BRIDGING THE ISTHMUS

The digging and construction of the Panama Canal make pretty grim reading. Not as grim perhaps as the history of Caribbean slavery, but similar in its epic scale of inhumanity, ruthless intent and loss of life. As the first Europeans to invade Central America, it was the Spanish who first saw the economic benefits of building a canal across the Isthmus of Panama to shorten routes to Peru...where they were actively engaged in plundering the riches of Inca civilisation and transporting them back to Spain.

By 1534, Spain's King Charles V had already looked into the feasibility of establishing a route across the isthmus with this thought in mind. But nothing came of it other than an improved terrestrial route – known as the Camino Real -- across the continental divide. Nor did later plans for the construction of a canal proposed by the explorer Alessandro Malaspina, following his expedition of 1788-93, produce any concrete results.

Scotland's abortive attempt to establish its Darien colony on the Caribbean side of the isthmus in 1698 toyed with similar hopes of mercantile activity between the two oceans. Launched in Edinburgh amidst great fanfare, the Darien Company was another effort to promote trade across the fifty-mile narrows. Excluded from commercial access to England's American colonies, Scottish investors (and their London bankers) saw this as a means of creating new business opportunities in the New World and of circumventing the embargo. By March 1700, however, the scheme had ended in disaster through a combination of poor planning and the lethal effects of tropical disease on the settlers.

It was not until 1855, when the Panama Railway

began operating, that the first integrated link connecting the Pacific and Atlantic oceans was established. Its impact on traffic between the eastern seaboard of the United States and California – spurred on by the Gold Rush of 1849 -- was enormous and proved a crucial factor in resurrecting interest in the concept of a man-made canal. Extending forty-eight miles from Colon to Panama City – and still operating to this day -- the railway would eventually play a critical role in the construction of the Panama Canal as well as determining the route which it would ultimately follow.

Fresh from his glorious Suez Canal project linking the Mediterranean to the Indian Ocean, the French developer and diplomat Ferdinand de Lesseps pioneered the first attempt at spanning the isthmus, in January 1880. His concept was a sea-level waterway (i.e. one without locks similar to the Suez Canal) through what was then the Colombian province of Panama in Central America. But the scheme was rushed and inadequate research into the region's complex hydrology and geology doomed it to eventual failure. A significant oversight in the French plan was the fact that sea levels on the Caribbean and Pacific coasts were not the same and could – had the project been completed – ultimately have led to unmanageable tidal flows.

Diseases like malaria and yellow fever added to these complications, killing vast numbers of labourers and key members of the French construction company. Ignorance of the mosquito's role as a carrier of these diseases further exacerbated the situation with unscreened hospital wards becoming virtual breeding grounds for these malevolent insects. Hostile working conditions on this scale made it virtually impossible to maintain an experienced work force and the skilled

117

engineers and managers recruited for this bold project fled back to France in fear of their lives. Dogged by disease and the difficulty of building a sea-level canal, plus a significant lack of French field experience in such climatic conditions, de Lesseps's scheme was eventually abandoned in 1893. But not before an estimated 21,000 workers had perished during the eight-year period of construction (1881–89). Understandably, this dramatic failure undermined investor support and did little to inspire confidence in the canal concept for some years to come.

By the turn of the century, however, fresh moves were afoot in Washington to mount a US venture as the economic and geopolitical importance of faster links beween America's Atlantic and Pacific coasts became more pressing. Initially, a route through Nicaragua was the preferred option. With large land holdings in Panama, however, the French Canal Syndicate successfully lobbied the US Congress to vote in favour of building a canal across Panama in an effort to offset some of the enormous losses incurred in their earlier project. But the skulduggery involved in this lobbying activity would become a source of acrimony between Panama and Washington for decades to come.

Having opted for a route through Panama, incumbent President Theodore Roosevelt focused his efforts on separating Panama from Colombian sovereignty and placing it under US control. This he largely achieved through military intervention as America's role on the world stage assumed more serious proportions. However, in 1921 – seven years after completion of the canal – America eventually agreed to pay Colombia reparations of $25 million in compensation for the territorial losses it suffered. In exchange, Colombia recognised Panamanian independence.

Work on the second canal project resumed on 4 June 1904 and included the purchase of all French equipment and sites for $25 million. Heading the operation was chief engineer John Frank Stevens (1905-1907) whose primary task was to develop an infrastructure capable of completing the canal. This consisted of rebuilding the Panama Railway and devising a rail-based soil disposal system to service the excavations. It also involved the construction of proper housing for canal workers as well as the development of extensive sanitation and mosquito-control programmes to eradicate yellow fever and other diseases from the Isthmus. Stevens also successfully argued the case against a sea-level canal similar to the French plan and, instead, persuaded President Theodore Roosevelt – an enthusiastic supporter of the canal project -- of the need to build a waterway incorporating both dams and locks.

A significant effort at eliminating disease, particularly yellow fever and malaria, was also made. The source of these maladies had originally been discovered in 1881 by Cuban scientist Dr Carlos Finlay who identified the mosquito as the carrier of the disease and whose theory and investigative work had recently been endorsed by Dr Walter Reed while in Cuba with the US Army during the Spanish-American War. With these diseases under control, and after major work on preparing the infrastructure, construction of an elevated canal with locks began in earnest.

As work progressed, the Americans gradually replaced the old French equipment with machinery designed for a larger scale of work (such as giant hydraulic crushers) which accelerated the pace of construction. Roosevelt later had the old French machinery minted into service medals for workers who had spent at least two years on the construction. They featured Roosevelt's likeness on the front with the name of the recipient and his years of service at the side, and an image of the Culebra Cut on the back of the medal.

In 1907, Roosevelt appointed George Washington Goethals as his new Panama Canal chief engineer. Work forged ahead and completion of the canal occurred two years ahead of schedule in 1914 and it was formally opened on 15 August 1914 with the passage of the freighter Ancon, an event somewhat overshadowed by the Great War in Europe. But advances in hygiene and medical science had resulted in a comparatively low death toll during the American construction phase. Nevertheless, 5,609 workers still died between 1904 and 1914 bringing the total death toll for the construction of the canal to a shocking 27,500.

By the 1930s, however, an inadequate water supply to feed the locks was becoming an issue for the canal's operating efficiency, which prompted the building of the Madden Dam across the Chagres River above Gatun Lake. Its completion in 1935 created Madden (later Alajuela) Lake, which provided additional water storage for the canal. In 1939, work began on a further major improvement: a new set of locks for the canal, large enough to carry the major warships that the US planned for future construction. This work continued for several years, and significant excavations were carried out on the new approach channels, but eventually terminated after the Second World War.

In the post-war years, American control of the canal and its surroundings became contentious as relations between Panama and the US grew increasingly fractious. Many Panamanians felt the canal zone belonged to Panama; while student protests prompted the Americans to fence in the zone and increase its *military presence. Negotiations towards a settlement begin in 1974 and resulted in the Torrijos-Carter Treaties. Signed by US President Jimmy Carter and Omar Torrijos of Panama on 7 September 1977, it set in motion the process of handing the canal over to Panamanian sovereignty on condition that Panama sign a treaty guaranteeing the permanent neutrality of the canal and allowing for a US return at anytime. Though controversial in America, the treaty led to full Panamanian control from 31 December 1999 with management of the canal transferring to the Panama Canal Authority.*

After the handover, Panama's government held an international bid to award a twenty-five-year contract for operation of the canal's container ports (chiefly two facilities at the Atlantic and Pacific outlets), which was won by Hutchison Whampoa, a Hong Kong-based shipping concern owned by international financier and industrialist Li Ka Shing, said to be the wealthiest Chinese in the world.

In September 2007, a $5.2 billion Panama Canal Expansion Project was launched with the potential to almost double the volume of cargo currently transiting the waterway by 2025. Completion is scheduled for 2014 and may coincide with the one-hundredth anniversary of the canal's construction. The plan involves: the construction of two new lock complexes – one on the Atlantic side and another on the Pacific side – each with three chambers; the excavation of new access channels to the new locks and the widening of existing navigation channels; and the deepening of the navigational channels and the increase of Gatun Lake's maximum operating depth.

This will allow a new breed of larger vessels to negotiate the canal. Existing Panamax dimensions accommodate ships of up to 294 metres (965 feet) in length, thirty-two metres width and twelve metres draft. The new Post-Panamax locks facilities – being constructed alongside the existing locks -- will take ships of up to 366 metres (1,200 feet), forty-nine metres width and fifteen metres draft. The present generation of Panamax vessels can transport up to 4,500 standard (TEU) containers; future Super Post-Panamax vessels will be capable of carrying up to 12,000 containers. Similarly, larger cruise ships and naval craft will be able to operate through the canal between the oceans.

Seventeen

As *Bella Mama* left the Panama Canal and sailed into the Pacific Ocean, Tad felt an immense weight lifted from his shoulders. Even as they descended the final flight of locks, he was struck by the warm, serene and inviting mood up ahead compared to the earlier grey, blustery conditions that prevailed when departing the Caribbean. This was his first captaincy and the passage through the canal had been an unmitigated disaster. But all the setbacks had been successfully overcome, he reasoned, and his vessel was now in the Pacific ready to cross this vast expanse of ocean towards the Galapagos, the Marquesas and other parts of French Polynesia. Despite some black marks, the youthful commander predicted better days ahead as his spirits soared on a wave of innocent euphoria.

This new-found optimism was short-lived, however, when next morning Chuck and Nicola announced their decision to jump ship and go back-packing in Costa Rica.

'We've had enough of the ship-board lifestyle,' complained Chuck. 'It's not what we expected and we're not altogether comfortable with the operation. We just can't face the prospect of another two months of uncertainty and anxiety getting *Bella Mama* to Tahiti and then on to Auckland.'

Tension gripped the vessel as heated words were exchanged between the Canadians. Accusations of disloyalty and unreliability erupted from Tad's side and of having lost confidence in the captain's judgement and professionalism from the other. Efforts by Ewan to pour oil on troubled waters were to no avail.

'There's no point undertaking a long trip in a small vessel with an unhappy crew,' he ventured diplomatically. 'It's probably better we know these things now rather than halfway across the Pacific.'

It seemed that just as Tad was beginning to decompress, his difficulties had returned with a vengeance. He turned an angry shade of pale white as his blood pressure rose. Boats and their engines can be fixed; but finding new and dependable crew for such a long voyage was not going to be easy. But at least the genie was out of the bottle. Ewan felt decidedly more comfortable now that the skipper knew of the couple's plan. For some time Chuck and Nicola had been confiding their intentions without actually reaching a decision or informing the boss. Ewan's earlier efforts at trying to dissuade them from abandoning a 'once-in-a-lifetime adventure and later regretting it' proved fruitless. The die was cast and the orderly chain-of-command slowly crumbling. While the adjacent Pacific waters momentarily induced an aura of tranquillity in the days that followed, the mood on board was anything but calm.

Once again, Tad disappeared ashore to telephone the owners and explain the latest piece of bad news. He returned some hours later and informed them that, given the latest developments, they were thinking of abandoning the Tahiti trip and selling *Bella Mama*. Adding to this, Tad announced that he'd received another job offer in California skippering a sixty-foot power yacht and was thinking of quitting.

Ewan digested all this over a pint of Balboa at the yacht club and tried to discern between the truths and half-truths of these latest developments: half the crew were quitting; the owners might sell the boat; and the captain was negotiating another job. As all these rats prepared to abandon ship, Ewan felt rather tipsy, somewhat saddened at these developments and just a tiny bit noble as *Bella Mama*'s only surviving crew.

He rowed back to the boat and, next morning, tuned

the boat's shortwave radio to the network of yachts scattered across the Pacific and listened to them describing local weather conditions and respective positions. Several British accents talked of motor-sailing towards the Galapagos due to a lack of wind. Others spoke of encountering whales and vast migrations of dolphins. Listening to their distant voices excited the imagination and made the prospect of abandoning this passage too painful to contemplate.

Tad re-appeared and soon made it clear that he shared these sentiments and really had no desire to abandon this unique sailing experience or waste all the plans he'd made to visit remote atolls in French Polynesia and, of course, to embellish his CV in the process. Ewan sensed from this news that a determined effort would be made to complete the passage and to hell with skippering a gin palace in California. This came as an immense relief.

On the verge of losing his compatriots to Costa Rica, Tad was now uncharacteristically chummy towards his only surviving crew member and even suggested an excursion into Panama City. As there were now only two of them remaining, it occurred to Ewan that Tad might be considering a two-man, trans-Pacific voyage as a pre-emptive solution to his problems. The thought -- and it was only a thought -- made him nervous. If Tad couldn't find crew replacements in Panama and was under pressure to get the boat to Tahiti, a quick departure could forestall any attempt by the owners to abandon the trip or sell the boat. Even at a hundred dollars a day, the prospect of compacting the workload of a four-man crew into a two-man team sounded dire. Ewan desperately wanted to navigate across this big ocean but as safely and comfortably as one could in a fifty-foot yacht. He concocted a few mental stalling tactics and smartened up for a night on the town.

THEY MOTORED ashore in the dinghy, jumped into a cab and headed for the night spots. Panama City – the Republic of Panama's capital – was only a few miles from Balboa at the Pacific end of the canal. Although it had Spanish architecture and baroque churches in its old *barrios*, the city's sprawling, sometimes shabby, modernity of high-rise apartment blocks and office skyscrapers predominated. The logos of global banking institutions like HSBC, Citibank, UBS, BNP and others brightened the night sky and proclaimed the city's newfound role as an offshore financial centre and Latin America tax haven.

After cruising the boulevards and dining on *tortillas,* the two men ended up at the Panama Hotel, one of the city's more salubrious establishments, where they listened appreciatively to live Latin American *salsa* music and watched elegant locals dancing in their well-polished, inimitable style. The women in Panama were voluptuous, shapely and by far the most attractive Ewan had seen anywhere in the Americas, north or south. There was absolutely no doubt, concurred the skipper, that they had more style than either their Caribbean or Gringo neighbours to the north.

Mindful of Tad's eye for the ladies and of their last outing in Jamaica, it occurred to Ewan that they could easily end up with another temporary crew member joining *Bella Mama.* This would certainly take his mind off the metaphorical ball, if not his own hyperactive *cojones.* Should this come to pass, however, any sudden departure for the Galapagos would undoubtedly be postponed, thus giving the owners time to have their say on how the vessel was to be deployed.

The only thing likely to prevent this happening that night was Tad's rather casual dress code. Wearing shorts, a tee-shirt and open-toe sandals was not the sort of sartorial chic normally associated with the *salsa* venues of upmarket Panama. In such attire, Tad looked more like a scruffy backpacker from north of the Rio Grande and, as such, not the kind of escort with whom these conservative *senoritas* would associate. Ewan chatted with a couple on the neighbouring table while Tad made various unsuccessful attempts to find a dance partner from the ample supply of unaccompanied ladies dotted around the ballroom.

Ewan discussed the transfer of canal ownership to Panamanian sovereignty and the end of what his neighbours called "the American occupation." President Carter – who negotiated this transfer to Panama in 1999 – undoubtedly handled things better than the British did over Suez Canal ownership in 1956, Ewan explained. Carter did, of course, have the benefit of their mistakes and the knowledge that his predecessor President Eisenhower had categorically refused to back the efforts of Britain, France and Israel at blocking Egypt's unilateral takeover from British control. This foreign policy debacle was the last time London dared embark on an independent military action without the blessings of Washington. Yet there were still many Americans who vilified the "peanut president" for succumbing to Panama's takeover demands.

While their conversation continued, Tad became increasingly frustrated at his inability to find a lady with whom to dance and could not understand why this was so. Normally, his good looks and lean physique guaranteed him considerable success with members of the opposite sex.

'Your problem is not your good looks,' Ewan volunteered, 'but your casual attire. Latinos scrub up well and look smart, especially when out dancing at

127

night. You look too much like a hippy Gringo and, frankly, you'll only make it with hookers in Latin America. That's my analysis. Prove me wrong.'

Tad shot him an angry glance and ordered another Balboa. To make his point, Ewan swaggered across the floor and invited a local beauty to dance. It was a high-risk strategy and certainly more likely to irritate than educate. But the *senorita* accepted – her name was Nina – and they spent the next half hour mingling with the dancers while Tad sulked over his beer on the sideline. Later, he explained why.

'I invited her in Spanish; I'm wearing slacks, shirt and shoes; and I look older and more respectable than you do. These girls have reputations to protect, you know. It's not rocket science. The local *hombres* are a jealous lot by nature and being seen dancing with a scruffy Gringo isn't good for any girl's reputation. Believe me.'

Fortunately, Tad grudgingly accepted this diagnosis and they returned to the boat unaccompanied by any of the lovely ladies. While his ego was somewhat dented...the local sisterhood remained unblemished and further on-board complications were avoided.

After a lazy Sunday anchored off the Balboa Yacht Club, the next day brought a change of team. Chuck and Nicola, having given their notice, were due to leave the boat that afternoon. Their departure was delayed over concerns about non-payment of salaries and getting air tickets back to Vancouver. Although angered by their breach of contract, the owners in Illinois paid up via bank transfer and the couple made a chilly exit.

Tad later admitted it was a bad idea inviting such unworldly people to crew on a trip like this. Nicola was a veritable powder keg on the verge of exploding whenever asked to do anything for fear of being shown wanting. Her partner, meanwhile, tended to avoid involvement in the rows and confrontations generated by his "princess". Tad said their departure, while inconvenient in operating terms, was probably a good thing, adding that he might have found a replacement.

Eighteen

The day after Chuck and Nicola's departure, Pierre – an affable young French Canadian from Montreal – joined the crew and immediately altered the mood on board. He seemed an altogether more mature and adult proposition than his predecessors. Initial impressions were of a confident 'dude' ready to make things work and get along with everybody. He said he'd been 'bumming around Costa Rica on a scooter' for the past three months and regaled them with tales of his adventures -- amorous and otherwise. It seemed that all the *senoritas* in Costa Rica wanted to marry French Canadians.

'What about other Canadians?' inquired Tad.

'Not a hope,' he laughed.

Apart from its women, enthused Pierre, Costa Rica – a neighbouring Central American republic -- had wonderful coastal and mountain scenery, no army 'to send innocent young boys to fight foreign wars for decadent old men' and much else to offer.

Next morning they sailed *Bella Mama* south to Flamenco Marina by following the long Amador Causeway that linked this new facility to the mouth of the canal. Having docked the boat, they found themselves in a beautiful location surrounded on all sides by evidence of change from the old US military infrastructure that once characterised the canal's approaches, to that of a more recreational ambience. The tree-lined causeway jutted out several miles from the mainland to Flamenco Island where a major new development including the marina, a cruise ship terminal and a large resort hotel with shopping arcades and restaurants was being built as part of the government's policy of exploiting Panama's abundant canal assets. The location offered spectacular views over the adjacent Gulf of Panama towards the thrusting skyline of Panama City. On either side of the approach road, sailing yachts lay at anchor either being readied for their sortie into the boundless Pacific or for navigating back along the canal into the Caribbean.

From the uncertainty and drama of recent days, Tad now seemed hell-bent on preparing *Bella Mama* for the vast distances and uncertainties that lay ahead. All concerns that he might resume his philandering ways and further delay this epic voyage now disappeared as they concentrated their efforts on acquiring victuals, water and fuel. Although the four-man crew had been reduced to three, one of whom was an unknown quantity in sailing terms, the consensus definitely favoured a speedy departure. The skipper was also keen to avoid any countermanding orders from the owners that might scupper his plans.

The first day was spent at Panama's largest food store – Super 99 – where the emphasis was on obtaining what the captain described as "dry goods" by which he meant cleaning materials and detergents. Day two was devoted to purchasing perishables such as eggs, dairy and meat produce. On the third day, they drove their rental car to an enormous municipal market and stocked up on a healthy selection of pulsars, fruit and vegetables. All this was later squirreled away in various nooks and crannies throughout the boat with meticulous attention to detail. According to Tad's culinary expertise, vegetables, fruit and eggs were best wrapped – item by item -- in newspaper and then carefully stored, mostly below deck under the saloon and cabin flooring. They were provisioned to the gunnels. In a more negative frame of mind, Ewan had visions of drifting across the mighty Pacific for months – without wind or engine – devouring huge quantities of rotting fruit.

The final task was to motor to the marina's fuel dock and take on diesel. This called for one hundred and eighty US gallons in the vessel's fuel tanks and another forty-eight gallons stored in eight six-gallon jerry cans to give them a total of 228 gallons. Three of the jerry cans were then lashed to the aft stanchions and the other five stowed in cockpit lockers. They also topped up the vessel's five fresh water tanks but expected to rely mainly on the water-maker – which converted salt water to fresh -- to supply most of their offshore needs.

The last few hours were spent feverishly making final phone calls and sending emails to loved ones. For all of them, this was like Columbus setting sail for the New World in 1492. After almost two weeks' delay in Panama, they were now keen to be on their way and to put the various engine and crew problems behind them. They'd enjoyed this stopover but it had caused further delays to those already incurred in Jamaica. So they fired up the Yanmar, cast off the warps, stowed the fenders and motored past the breakwater before heading south into the buoyed channel beyond Flamenco Island.

They were, it seemed, finally on their way. The great adventure was about to start…and the mood was decidedly upbeat. Ewan prayed for fair winds and good weather…and took a last, lingering look at Panama City's imposing skyline across the bay. A neon HSBC logo winked faintly on the skyline against the deep purple of an evening sky.

Then – as if by some well-orchestrated act of God – the air was dramatically rent by a torrent of high-octane expletives emanating from the cockpit. Ewan winced as the foul language echoed across the water on such a perfect evening. The incongruity was painful.

'Our fuckin' engine's overheating,' screamed the

demented captain. 'The gauge is reading one-twenty degrees. It should be eighty centigrade. We have to go back.'

The duty helmsman swung the wheel to port in response to the order and they motored pathetically back to the jetty, stunned by this latest set-back. Already the skipper's forehead was embossed with shining beads of perspiration. This yacht and its captain were definitely not getting along, thought Ewan.

That weekend, the crew drifted into a mindless limbo amply lubricated with Balboa lager and white rum *seco tonica* cocktails. And then, as if to heighten the drama, Tad announced that he was resigning his captaincy of *Bella Mama* and accepting the job in California. Terrific news, thought Ewan: the crew and captain jump ship leaving one beleaguered Brit and a Canadian backpacker to get this doomed Yankee sloop to Tahiti. Ewan weighed his options: to stay or not to stay…and thought of himself as a nautical Hamlet. At the same time he wondered if Tad didn't concoct phantom job offers like this as a psychological buffer to save face and cope with failure.

Once again, Tad had to divulge bad news to his distant owners. Once again his soul would be nagged by a sense of failure and low self-esteem. In doing so, though, he again deviously failed to disclose his own rather pertinent intentions. This time, the owner – Tom Morgate – asked to speak to Ewan. But before he could utter a word, the affable Brit politely declared unequivocally that *Bella Mama* was unfit for purpose; the craft had not been adequately overhauled to the standard required for a long ocean passage into the lonely waters of the South Pacific, one of the remotest parts of the planet. Owner and captain must equally share responsibility, he said.

'That's why I hire a fuckin' captain,' erupted the

crusty curmudgeon from the other end of the line.

Having regained composure, he then went on to extol the excellence of the skipper's sailing skills. In reality, though, Tad's management style left much to be desired. And the present imbroglio was being compounded by his failure to come clean about the California offer or -- latest revelation -- that he intended to resign and fly there for an interview.

In the midst of such confusion and with the likelihood of *Bella Mama* staying in Panama for several more weeks, Ewan decided it was time to fly back to Florida to find a hurricane hole for *Contigo*. The voyage to Tahiti would soon be a month behind schedule and – assuming the Pacific leg actually materialised – there could be further delays in the weeks ahead. This meant the Caribbean's summer hurricane window would be wide open by the time his crewing obligations to Papeete terminated, leaving *Contigo* in the lap of the weather gods. Marine insurance imposed strict conditions on boat owners and one of them was certainly not to go cavorting across the Pacific Ocean on somebody else's vessel.

Ewan called Tom in Illinois and explained his plight, reminding him of their agreement that, in such an event, he'd pay his air fare to Fort Lauderdale and back. Tom agreed and Ewan flew out of Panama's Tucuman International Airport for Miami next morning.

On parting, Tad was adamant that he wanted him to return and continue the passage to Tahiti once he'd sorted out *Contigo*. Ewan assured him he would come back but decided, privately, that it was really Tad's responsibility to stage-manage his own exit should he so desire and not his. What might or might not be going on in the captain's convoluted mind was his business.

Nineteen

Things moved fast when Ewan got back to Panama a few weeks later. The skipper met him at Tucuman International Airport on a Sunday morning and immediately began unburdening his frustrations at the slow progress of engine repair work now being undertaken by the local Yanmar agent. Language problems had caused confusion with the local mechanics, he explained, as they struggled to remove the engine and truck it back to their workshop. Once again, their conversation plunged into the three-cornered dynamics of *Bella Mama*, the owner and its captain. It was the start to what became a rather pivotal first day back in Panama.

As they made their way through the city's busy streets, Tad drove like a maniac and eventually crashed his rental car into a city bus. He was, as the bus driver forcefully pointed out, totally at fault. They spent the next two hours at the centre of a chaotic traffic jam that developed around their *contretemps* waiting for traffic cops to appear. It had brought down-town Panama City to a virtual standstill; but they needed a police report for the rental firm's insurance. Otherwise, they would have to pay for repairs to both the bus and their car. After much debate, this was eventually concluded and they continued their journey in driving rain back to the boat at Flamenco Marina. Already there was a mood of foreboding in the air. Over a fortnight had elapsed since Ewan left the boat and – for reasons beyond his ken – the engine was still not fixed. He climbed back onto *Bella Mama* and exchanged a few Gallic salutations with Pierre.

Night fell and the rain lashed down. There was a big storm brewing in the southwest. Tad invited them to join him at the dockside bar for cocktails where they chatted for some time. Then out of the dark and into the shelter of the bar's thatched roof stumbled Bob, a live-aboard electrician from Texas. He joined them. Bob did odd-job repairs for transiting yachts and had been anchored in the bay on the west side of the causeway for almost a year. In recent weeks, explained Pierre, he'd been doing work projects for Tad who clearly liked him a lot. Bob claimed poverty 'on account of deevorse and a cheatin' wife' so they bought him drinks and showed sympathy. He'd also survived a prolonged battle with leukaemia and felt lucky to be alive and still have possession of his boat after an ugly marital meltdown. It was obvious from his drawn features and rain-soaked hair that these weather conditions were not to his liking. When the downpour eased, Bob disappeared into the night while *Bella Mama*'s crew continued chatting amongst themselves and flirting with the barmaids.

The storm grew in intensity and began to threaten a handful of boats anchored on the windward side of the causeway. They went to the rescue of a French yacht with a solo caretaker crew on board which was dragging anchor and likely to end up impaled on the dangerous rocks along the shore. The owner, it seemed, had flown back to Paris for a couple of weeks and left a young backpacker from Bordeaux on board as a make-do security guard. Unfortunately, his watchman knew precious little about boats…not even how to start the engine. Darkness fell and Ewan fetched their rental car and directed its powerful headlights onto the rain-swept drama while Tad swam out and climbed aboard the pitching vessel, its transom now only fifty feet from the jagged rocks.

Eventually, he got the motor going and instructed the terrified backpacker on how to haul up the anchor and then motor-sailed the vessel into the inky darkness to find a safer anchorage. Pierre and Ewan returned to *Bella Mama* – comfortably docked within the marina – and, after drying down and changing clothes, mixed a couple of *seco tonicas* and awaited the skipper's return. By the time the storm abated and Tad climbed back on board, it was well past midnight and they analysed the night's proceedings before retiring to their bunks.

Early next morning when Tad returned ashen-faced from his morning jog, however, they learnt that a more terrible drama had been unfolding elsewhere as they fought to save the French sailboat from crashing onto the rocks. A naked body had been found among the rocks in the small Playita Bay on the west end of the causeway, he said. It was the body of a white male and had a frayed twelve-foot length of heavy rope tied around its waist. He thought it was the body of Texas Bob. A waiter at the nearby beach restaurant had asked Tad to come back later after the police arrived to see if he could positively identify the Gringo's corpse. It was floating face-down among the flotsam and jetsam at the rocky end of this popular local beach. Tad was pale and badly shaken.

After breakfast, they wandered back across the road towards Playita where the flashing strobe of a police car indicated that the authorities had arrived. Tad and Pierre – who had socialised and worked closely with Texas Bob in recent weeks – were asked if they knew who it was. They confirmed that it was Bob and that he lived aboard a ketch called *Orion*. Both were appalled, however, at the lack of decorum and respect shown by the police for the deceased as they "joked among themselves and dragged the body onto the beach like a dead fish." The face was bloated and shockingly disfigured by rock abrasions. Their attitude suggested either contempt for Gringos, a culture of police brutality or – more likely – their own Anglo-Saxon

137

sensitivities about death. Either way, it was not a pleasant experience and left a bad taste.

Piecing together what might or might not have happened to Bob became an obsession within the group. It seemed that the previous afternoon, he'd hitched a ride ashore in a passing friend's dinghy. But when the storm blew up and their battle to save the French yacht got underway, Bob had no way of getting back to *Orion*. Clearly, he was concerned that -- like most other skippers anchored out that night -- his boat might drag its anchor and drift onto the rocks. But the questions uppermost in most minds were: why was this frayed length of rope around his waist and why was he naked? In short, what was he trying to achieve that led to this dreadful ending?

To complicate matters further, after the storm abated that night, a patrolling coastguard vessel had apparently discovered *Orion* unmanned and dragging its anchor towards the rocks. To save it from destruction, they had towed and re-anchored the vessel in safer waters oblivious to the drama that had recently unfolded. By this time, the group deduced that Bob had already met his fate and that his body was by now drifting across Playita Bay towards the beach.

In the end, they could only conclude that this hapless mariner – instead of interrupting their rescue operations with the French yacht and seeking assistance – had found a length of rope on the shore, tied one end around his waist and the other to a fixture, removed his jeans to lighten his load and attempted to swim out to the ketch; in short, to go it alone and save his boat. The rope, they presumed, was to act as a lifeline back to shore should he risk being over-whelmed by the stormy conditions. The only flaw in this theory, however, was that no trace of the rope's other extremity or of Bob's clothing could be found onshore. And how did this twelve-foot length of rope around his waist come to be severed?

Another theory – equally unsubstantiated – was that Bob had swum out to *Orion;* found his anchor entangled with some underwater object; tied a short length of rope around his waist and attached it cursorily to a cleat; and dived overboard to try and remove the obstruction. Given that Bob was not in good health, he then became entangled in underwater lines and drowned in the process.

Whatever had happened, Bob's unexplained death left a heavy pall hanging over the crew of *Bella Mama*. Tad and Pierre were not only badly shaken by the whole experience but also by the protracted process of police questioning and the lurid forensic identification attending such a tragedy.

But this was small beer compared to the next storm about to explode about Captain Tad's badly bruised cranium: in a name, Lavinia Morgate -- proprietor of *Bella Mama* -- a blue-rinse dame from America's Deep South with her own very particular agenda and priorities.

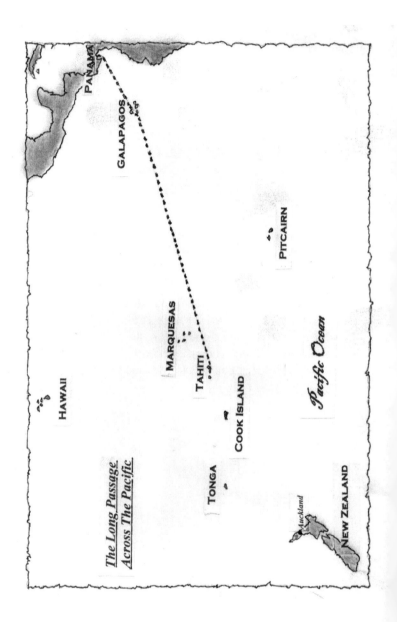

The Long Passage Across The Pacific

PANAMA

GALAPAGOS

PITCAIRN

MARQUESAS

TAHITI

HAWAII

COOK ISLAND

Pacific Ocean

TONGA

Auckland

NEW ZEALAND

Twenty

Into this grim scene parachuted the feisty seventy-nine-year old owner's wife on an unannounced visit from southern Illinois. Her mood was abrasive and jarred horribly after the sadness felt about Texas Bob's grisly death. But it was hardly surprising. Her boat had been in Panama for many weeks and she had finally come down to investigate. She was obviously unhappy at the constant delays and expense incurred in repairing *Bella Mama's* engines. She was also decidedly unimpressed on the day she arrived at her crew's absence and involvement in the police investigations into Bob's death and, as such, ready for combat.

'Why in Jesus's name are you concerned with such matters?' she demanded when Tad and Pierre returned. 'I pay my captain and crew to look after *Bella Mama,* not to get mixed up with the local cops.'

Tears welled up in Tad's weary eyes as he tried, in vain, to explain the sad circumstances of their absence. But there was little he could say against such a harsh barrage of interrogation At five feet tall, Lavinia Morgate may have had the bearings of a pocket-sized grandmother but her persona was large, assertive and vocal. As such, she presented a comical yet paradoxical spectre in this glitzy Panamanian marina. Of slim build, she wore a long flowery cotton dress that almost reached her ankles, white socks and even whiter sneakers. Her complexion, too, was shiny white – almost ceramic – offset by stark blue eyes and straight, shoulder-length peroxide hair. Her voice was shrill and modulated by an over-egged Southern accent that left no doubt about her affiliations. She may have been from southern Illinois – a northern state -- but her style, vocabulary and opinions were unmistakably Old Southern. And it was soon very obvious that this tough old dame meant business. Tad's Wicked Witch and nemesis had arrived…

The next few days were not easy for the captain. The owners had clearly lost confidence in his ability to manage the vessel's maintenance requirements. Lavinia commandeered the rental car – 'Godammit I'm paying for it' – and re-deployed Ewan as her Spanish-speaking chauffeur. In addition to finding his way around Panama City and adapting to its brisk traffic culture, he now had to assist in relocating her ladyship from a swanky downtown Marriott to an equally imposing hostelry located on the nearby banks of the Panama Canal.

It was now obvious that Tad was going to be under much closer scrutiny by his owners. Ewan, meanwhile, was transformed into a driver, porter, interpreter and sounding-board to a very disgruntled proprietor. This was a tricky role because he had no intention of becoming either spy or quisling. Instead, he adopted the role of the discreet British butler: an ageing Jeeves in shorts and tee-shirt equipped – as and when needed -- with skills in Barcelona Spanish. Privately, he fantasised about jumping ship, obtaining Panamanian citizenship and morphing into a slick taxi-driver ferrying wealthy Americans around the isthmus…but then thought better of it.

As Tad bluffed and bumbled his way through explanations of what had been happening over the past weeks in Panama – mercifully coinciding with Ewan's absence in Florida – Lavinia gradually formed the impression of someone in her employ with limited management skills. This saw Ewan become both interpreter and negotiator between Yanmar's agents and this diminutive old lady with the high-decibel voice about what to do with her boat. Ewan pinned down the options and negotiated, as a sort of linguistic intermediary, with the various protagonists repairing the generator and the main engine. But what, he kept wondering, had been happening during the past few weeks of his absence?

Each morning thereafter, he dutifully picked up his charge at the hotel and drove her to *Bella Mama's* slip in the marina where she was deferentially ushered aboard by her captain and the inquisition would resume.

'Goddamit Tad, how is it possible that both the Yanmar and the generator engines are *kaput*?' she demanded. 'Why weren't they thoroughly overhauled in Fort Lauderdale? What the hell were you doing all those weeks in the Summerfield yard?'

Life now became a bizarre cocktail of Lavinia's gushing bonhomie towards her chauffeur and Tad's dark forebodings about his employment prospects. The owners had obviously lost faith in their captain. To some extent this was merited and the product of long-term maintenance oversights which Tad, in his bid to please these penny-pinching owners, had brushed under the carpet. The entire mood was increasingly fraught as the old lady's pent-up fury focused on the captain.

Next morning Ewan was invited up to Lavinia's hotel suite and given the phone to speak to her husband in Illinois. Would he be prepared to take over as captain with Tad staying on as first mate? he asked. Already anticipating this proposition, his response was swift and succinct:

'I'd only do so with Tad's concurrence and cooperation. And I'm not crossing the Pacific Ocean without another experienced sailor on board either as a member of the crew or as the skipper.'

'But we've completely lost confidence in Tad's judgement,' explained Tom, 'even though he's a damn good sailor. Do you mind, at least, sounding him out on this matter?'

This Ewan agreed to do knowing full well that Tad's pride would be so injured at such a demotion, or even the suggestion of such a demotion, that he would never accept. Ewan also knew that his sailing skills – both as captain and crew – were no match for Tad's. This was further endorsed by one of the Canadian's former bosses who – by a stroke of amazing good fortune -- happened to be passing through the Panama Canal en route to Baja California as these dramas unfolded.

'From my experience,' he explained over a discrete dinner one night, 'Tad served as an excellent member of crew and first mate.'

'Precisely,' said Lavinia, 'as a first mate he was excellent but not as a captain.'

Ewan was now becoming a bridge between these two unhappy protagonists and began to tire of the whole messy affair. Despite the rancour and squabbling, though, his desire to sail across the Pacific remained strong. After months of preparation, Tad had similar aspirations and clung to the hope that this delivery to New Zealand – and his captaincy – would survive and that names like Tahiti and the Galapagos would become a reality and not a dream.

Work on the boat now accelerated as *Bella Mama* was hauled and her bottom cleaned and anti-fouled in readiness for the long voyage ahead. Several leaking through-hulls were repaired and her Maxi-prop greased. More important, though, the overheating difficulties afflicting the generator-set and the Yanmar were, it seemed, largely resolved.

But the delicate matter of Tad swapping roles with his first mate had yet to be broached. Next evening over cocktails the opportunity for a private *tete-à-tete* arose and, as he'd suspected, the Canadian erupted with derision and indignation at the mere suggestion of demotion or of Ewan assuming the skipper's role. As he calmed down, however, Ewan reminded him of two important considerations if he accepted the owners' proposition: first, that he would realise a dream and fulfil his trans-pacific goal; and secondly, that he would avoid the risk of being sacked and getting a black mark on his resume on his first professional captaincy.

'Why not keep your head down, suffer the indignities and then show your worth once we're at sea,' he reasoned. 'In that way you keep your job and may even be re-instated as skipper somewhere down the line. I'd certainly be quite comfortable with that arrangement.'

But Tad, not without reason, would definitely not be. He lashed out in all directions and showed little gratitude for the support given to him thus far *vis-à-vis* the Morgates. Next morning, Ewan passed on this reaction to Lavinia who fulminated about her captain's character flaws and then called her husband in Illinois.

'Once an asshole, always an asshole,' she roared down the line to Tom after updating him on Tad's reaction. Ewan was then ordered to leave the room and wait downstairs in the lobby while they discussed their options.

Half an hour later Lavinia emerged from the lift.

'Tom wants him fired immediately. So drive me to the YMCA Travel Agency. I need to buy a one-way ticket to Miami for his return flight to Florida. Tomorrow morning I want you to pick me up at seven-thirty and take me to the boat. Tad will be dismissed and off *Bella Mama* with all his possessions by eleven o'clock. Then you'll drive him to the airport.'

The speed of change was both shocking and awful as Ewan wrestled with the full implications of what was happening. That night he cooked a beef stew in the galley and reflected on the skipper's impending fate. Not for the first time, he felt pangs of sympathy at his plight. Why was he being so obstinate when there was so much at stake? There was an exit strategy, if only he would swallow his pride and accept it.

According to Lavinia, Tad was a 'passive-aggressive type.' Although not quite sure what this meant, Ewan took it to be a negative characteristic because she and Tom now seemed to demonise their captain at every opportunity. They were also critical of his spendthrift use of the credit cards assigned for managing the boat's operating costs. Tad was apparently unable to account for nearly $7,000 worth of expenditures that he'd incurred, mostly through ATM cash withdrawals and for which he had no receipts. Ewan wondered if, feeling guilty about Tad's dismissal, they were over-egging his shortcomings in order to salve their consciences. At such moments, human beings could be most unattractive.

Next morning Ewan rose early from his tiny cabin and prepared for what promised to be an unpleasant day. Tad was nowhere to be seen having failed to return to the boat from his evening jog. He picked up Lavinia at the appointed hour from the hotel and drove her in silence to the boat. By the time they reached *Bella Mama,* Tad had materialised from whatever nocturnal activities kept him ashore and was now standing in the cockpit. He was promptly ordered below deck and into the aft cabin where his notice was served. A brief altercation ensued and voices were raised; then Tad emerged pale and tense and began gathering up his effects.

The indignity and humiliation were too painful to witness for the remaining crew. To Pierre and Ewan – mere recreational sailors at best – this no more than a wonderful voyage of self-discovery and an opportunity to explore distant shores. To Tad, however, it was a huge setback on a career path he'd been following for over a decade. For his first command to end like this was perverse and terrible. But what on earth had been happening on *Bella Mama* during those weeks when he was off the payroll in Florida?

Pierre and Ewan wandered round the sprawling marina with its chic shops, designer clothes, chandleries, yacht brokers and restaurants not sure of what was going to happen next. Would the passage to New Zealand be aborted and *Bella Mama* sold? Would a new captain be imported? Or would the first mate be promoted to captain and a new experienced sailor recruited? While Tad packed his rucksack and made his painful exit, morale hit bottom and they floated in an uncomfortable limbo. With the death of Texas Bob and now Tad's dismissal – coupled with the engine failures negotiating the canal and the desertion of Nicola and Chuck – Panama had been a bitter-sweet experience in more ways than one.

Once packed and off the boat, Tad declined a ride to the airport saying he had been offered a lift by someone else. Later that evening, though, they were somewhat surprised to meet him at the local marina bar?

'What happened, Tad?' asked Ewan. 'Did you miss your flight?'

'No, I re-scheduled the ticket. I'm staying on in Panama with friends.'

'Not our agent Tania by any chance?'

'You could be right,' he said.

'What's the plan?'

'I've got a passage to Australia on another sailboat.'

'As the skipper?'

'Wouldn't you like to know.'

Next morning Ewan collected Lavinia at the usual

time with orders, on this occasion, to take her to a local hairdresser. Her luminous blond hair needed another chemical work-over. Later, as they drove along the palm-fringed Amador Causeway, out of the bright morning mist suddenly loomed the tall, dangly figure of Tad on his morning jog. Ewan peeped the horn and waved. Tad waved back and, with a big smile, proffered the middle-finger of disrespect.

It was the last he ever saw of the boy from Horse Fly who'd given the 'old fart' such a fabulous break at a difficult time in life and for which he would always be very grateful. *Vaya con dios, capitano*, he muttered and drove on.

Twenty-one

After an uneventful weekend at the Flamenco Yacht Club, Ewan drove along the causeway to Lavinia's hotel on Monday morning to see what surprises her ladyship had in store for what remained of the crew. She emerged from the building in a floppy straw hat and the usual sartorial mix of flowery frock and sneakers. Once in the car, he was instructed to drive to Tucumen International Airport on the other side of Panama City. A new captain had been found, she explained, and he was due to arrive from Florida in a few hours' time. The only thing she knew about him was 'that he's a professional delivery captain, that he's Swedish and that his name is Ove Bergengren.' Things were beginning to happen...and the prospects for seeing the Galapagos and French Polynesia improving by the hour.

They met the new skipper off an American Airlines flight from Fort Lauderdale and, after formal introductions, drove him back to Panama City. In his early fifties, he seemed personable and exuded an air of self-confidence born, no doubt, of countless transatlantic crossings and other impressive yacht deliveries to his credit. After lunch at the Marriot, they made their way back along the Amador Causeway to Isla Flamenco and *Bella Mama.* Already Ewan sensed a more intelligent approach to the way things were discussed and considered which, under the prevailing circumstances, came as a relief. Unlike the earlier crew, the age bias was now shifting towards an older cast of characters. Perhaps there were advantages to being old after all.

During the next few days, he continued in his role as her ladyship's chauffeur, gofer and interpreter interspersed with the occasional request for advice on things like clothing for long voyages, toys for grandchildren and suntan cream for ceramic complexions. Lavinia was a fickle old duck with mood-swings oscillating from insipid sweetness to dark paranoia...but there were glimpses of good-natured common sense beginning to peep through the dark clouds.

The new captain, after a rapid assessment of his new command, decided the boat's fuel capacity was inadequate, so he and Ewan set off in the rental car in search of two fifty-gallon oil drums in what turned out to be the rougher parts of Puerto de Balboa. His plan was to extend *Bella Mama*'s fuel range by lashing two of these drums to her after-quarters in order to store an additional hundred gallons of diesel.

Eventually, two plastic Texaco drums were located in a ramshackle docklands workshop on the waterfront which he purchased for twenty-five dollars each. Later, they were slotted neatly between the yacht's two backstays – a perfect fit – and very skilfully lashed in place.

Next day, the new leader said he wanted to depart as soon as possible and asked Ewan, in effect, to keep the Wicked Witch out of his hair while he focused on more pressing tasks. It occurred to him, though, that his role as butler and *aid de camp* was not going to sit comfortably with their new captain for much longer. It could even come to be resented. As Lavinia's minder, however, this tiresome duty had to be tolerated if he was to remain part of the trans-Pacific crew. The whole scenario – along with her bawdy manner and tedious Southern drawl -- added an almost surreal dimension to proceedings.

What had not yet been made clear at this juncture was whether Lavinia would be sailing from Panama aboard *Bella Mama* or flying out to join them in Tahiti.

Ewan's occasional probes on the subject proved fruitless.

'Will you be leaving with us from Panama?' he asked delicately.

'You'll be the first to know, honey, when I've decided.'

'It might be best to tell the captain first,' he ventured.

'Yes sir, I think you might be right. But first things first.'

By mid-June – after two-and-a-half expensive months in Panama – it seemed as if *Bella Mama* was finally getting ready for another departure. Would she this time escape the tenacious hold this place had held over the benighted Hylas? Or was some other jinx lurking up ahead to force them back to Flamenco Island?

After a day of intense activity fuelling and buying provisions, they concentrated on keeping Lavinia's unpredictable mind focused on a list of tasks she had to perform before leaving; if indeed she was to leave. These included despatching Tad's final accounts back to Tom in Illinois, followed by visits to the bank, the post office and the pharmacy. They then drove to Panama City to pay the local Yanmar agency's hefty bill for the engine repair work. Afterwards, Ewan was instructed to find a grocery store where Lavinia could purchase a crate of peach juice drinks. This was the first indication that she might actually be planning to sail with them when they departed in a few hours' time. Final confirmation occurred when she settled the marina accounts for *Bella Mama* and then asked to be driven back to the hotel to check out and for her bags to be transferred to the boat.

Elsewhere, the new captain and Pierre accelerated progress on a long list of chores still to be performed before casting off. As the sun settled in the west, they returned the rental car, politely bundled Lavinia into her stern state room and then motor-sailed out of the marina into a huge flotilla of well-lit merchant vessels waiting to make the east-bound shuttle through the canal. After so many false starts on this the most daunting leg of their ocean crossing, the exit from Flamenco Island seemed almost prosaic. It was ten o'clock. Two months earlier, when first trying to escape Panama's tenacious grip, they had been hyped to the eyeballs in anticipation of the exciting passage upon which they were about to embark. By contrast, tonight's departure under The Swede's command seemed more like a day-outing on the Solent than the start of a trans-Pacific crossing.

But at last they were resuming the voyage to Tahiti. Ewan was the only survivor of the original Florida team that had begun this eventful delivery from Fort Lauderdale back in March. It was seventy-eight days since they'd dropped anchor off Puerto Cristobal at the Atlantic end of the canal. Fortunately, he'd been able to escape Tad's disintegrating regime for some weeks in order to prepare *Contigo* for the hurricane season in Florida.

THEY SAILED westwards for the next two days along Panama's Pacific coast to a headland called Punta Mala, encountering strong currents on the way, and then set a course of two-thirty-two degrees out across the world's biggest ocean towards the Galapagos Archipelago. The sky was clear and they had a ten-knot wind on the nose. When it veered a few degrees, they picked up an extra knot of speed and motor-sailed; at which point Tad's ghost returned to haunt *Bella Mama* as her engine started over-heating again.

But this time they rapidly located and bypassed the

raw water blockage problem, cut out a flattened hose length, opened the valve and cheered as raw water once again blurted out of the transom exhaust and cooled the over-heating Yanmar. They resumed passage and, for the third night since quitting Panama, Ewan cooked dinner and settled down for another night sail. Tedium would be the greatest challenge on this long passage to Tahiti. The experience, as he drifted into sleep, would either rid him of the yachting bug forever or turn him into an addict. *Bella Mama* battled into an unyielding wind and thumped hard on breaking waves.

After a good night's sleep from midnight to six o'clock, his mind was refreshed as dawn broke. He was on the helm from six to nine o'clock. The sea was choppier and the wind still infuriatingly on the nose. He adjusted the autopilot four degrees off wind on a course of two-fourteen degrees and eased the Genoa to achieve an occasional one-knot improvement to a speed of five-point-three knots. Meanwhile, the Yanmar purred contentedly at twenty-two-hundred revolutions per minute and the heat gauge stayed at eighty-two degrees Celsius. The apparent wind speed was seventeen knots, which was brisker than usual.

They had already completed about one-third of the 874-nautical mile passage to the Galapagos. The GPS told them there was another 597 miles to the Darwin Anchorage. Progress was relatively slow but the skipper wanted to work the engine at what he calculated to be the most economical speed in order to avoid further problems and maximise fuel efficiency 'even if it adds a few days to our trip.' At a hundred dollars a day why should one complain? said Ewan.

After completing his watch, the *jeune homme* from Quebec – instead of getting some sleep -- tuned into a shortwave network on the single-side-band radio and chatted away in French about weather conditions being experienced by Francophone vessels scattered across the ocean. The French hams seemed more active in this part of the world than the Anglophones which may have had a lot to do with the trickle of French and French Canadian vessels plying across the Pacific to and from French Polynesia. Earlier, there had been much evidence of this Gallic traffic at various marinas, anchorages and yacht clubs along the canal where French sometimes vied with Spanish as the *lingua franca*.

Ove, meanwhile, wrestled constantly with *Bella Mama*'s sails in a battle between speed-over-the-ground and rhumb-line deviation. With seventeen-knot winds to contend with he was not having much success. The mainsail and Genoa sheets were tensioned to a ferocious extent and the hull was ploughing into a strong wind as the oncoming seas burst over the decks. Birdlife – the occasional flight of gulls and terns -- slowly disappeared as they headed deeper into the Pacific and away from land.

Then, at precisely nine o'clock one morning, their senior resident and proprietor – Princess Lavinia -- emerged from her state-room in a radiant aura of smiles, good nature and snow-blond hair. After several days of solitude punctuated by occasional bouts of retching seasickness, Lavinia had come out to tell her employees that she was still very much alive and reading one book a day. It seemed that one of her ample suitcases was packed with reading matter – mostly on psychiatry and biographies – and that she was well acquainted with long ocean passages. They learnt more about the owner every day. She fried herself a pork chop, an egg and a half-raw slice of potato for breakfast in the galley and then returned to her state-room.

On Friday -- one of many Fridays – the weather

conditions deteriorated and *Bella Mama* was overtaken by a brisk rainstorm that made the rest of the day bumpy and uncomfortable as she lurched over conflicting wave patterns. Once again the lee-cloth collapsed and Ewan crashed to the deck of his tiny cabin in a helpless heap: another rude awakening. But spirits improved as the weather cleared. The mood on board remained convivial, but tedium – partly induced by a boundless expanse of sea and sky -- occasionally nagged at the conscious mind until it wandered off on some other tangent. Hopefully, interesting stopovers would provide worthwhile antidotes to such unwelcome moods.

The captain, meanwhile, regaled his crew with quick-fire homilies that were obviously aimed at displaying wisdom, wit and knowledge, all with varying degrees of success. His style was emerging as one of 'let's get there as soon as possible' with little concern for crew safety or interest in maintaining a ship's log. But the owner seemed to approve of him and was clearly relieved at being underway after seventy-eight costly days languishing in Panama.

Progress, though, was slow with the wind still on *Bella Mama*'s nose and a propeller – according to The Swede – whose blades were under-pitched and generating a mere three-knots of forward propulsion. With four hundred and seventy-five nautical miles to the Galapagos, they were not yet halfway to their first Pacific destination nor were they making much headway. Ewan completed the crossword puzzle in a back issue of the *Miami Herald* and then resumed progress on Gibbon's daunting *Decline and Fall.*

Twenty-two

They sailed across the Pacific with all sense of time dictated by meals, watches, daylight and darkness. Ewan's night shift on this particular day – June twenty-second – was from twenty-one hours to midnight. This allowed time for a good night's sleep until 06.00 hours when he resumed helm duties. The morning slot was particularly appealing because it was at this time of day, as the sun rose and the air warmed, that his mind felt alert and refreshed.

At six-thirty the GPS said they were exactly four hundred nautical miles from the Galapagos which he noted in his diary. Another benefit of the dawn watch was having the cockpit to oneself so that random thoughts could be scribbled down uninterrupted with pen and pad perched on knees. On this occasion, his journal noted that the engine had been running almost non-stop at 2,200 RPMs since departing Panama five days earlier. The freezer – normally, a big drain on the vessel's house batteries -- received a one-hour operating boost every eight hours from the generator which seemed to keep the boat's ample supply of steaks and *charcuterie* adequately frozen and other items in the adjacent refrigerator sufficiently chilled.

Later, the sea state turned choppy and uncomfortable with night-time conditions "rather grotty" with progress over the previous twenty-four hours amounting to less than a hundred nautical miles. His port-side bunk was now rather precarious with a strong risk of tipping its contents onto the cabin floor as *Bella Mama* assumed a port tack and confronted chunky waves. He retreated to a spare slot in the saloon and wedged himself comfortably on a sofa bench to get some sleep.

But that night Ove decided to stop the engine as the

wind conditions improved. The sudden silence seemed abrupt and almost deafening. Without the Yanmar to smother background noises, his ears and mind gradually re-focused on every sound the boat and sea created which made sleeping difficult. The whole mental image of a tiny fibreglass shell like *Bella Mama* adrift in such a vast ocean hundreds of miles from land conjured up alarming thoughts if left unchecked. It was much better to ring down a curtain of sleep, thought Ewan, or concentrate on the more heroic aspects of the adventure.

Some time later, Ove restarted the engine but then, after ten minutes, shut it down again; the Yanmar was still over-heating. No raw water was being expelled from the exhaust, which probably explained why this was happening.

'Could it be the raw water pump impeller?' Ewan asked. 'They only last for a certain amount of time.'

Ove dismantled the pump chamber, removed the covering plate and reported that the little rubber impeller wheel which sucks water from the sea and pushes it through the engine's cooling ducts was "shot." The mangled remains of the old one had to be removed and a new copy eased onto the fulcrum. Normally, this was a pretty straightforward, if fiddly, job on marine engines. Despite the best efforts of captain and crew, however, this particular impeller refused to dislodge and they sailed on into the night without a motor. The engine's poor housing design and the inaccessibility of the cooling pump made this a difficult task, particularly at three o'clock in the morning.

Next day, Lavinia emerged early and cooked herself a steak for breakfast before calling her husband in Illinois on the satellite phone. She'd not been seen for several days but her commanding tone reminded them of who was paying the bills... as well as the vessel's rather poor showing since leaving Fort Lauderdale. Her conversation with Tom was largely confined to a report on the vessel's progress and performance and on what an excellent job the new captain was doing. Curiously, no mention was made of the engine problems. Here they were, halfway between Panama and the Galapagos, without an engine to keep their victuals fresh or the propeller turning and Lavinia omits to brief her financial backer on this salient point. They assumed from this oversight that she didn't want to cause her husband any more concern about the boat than necessary...and that there wasn't much he could do to help, anyway.

Hopefully, there were repair facilities in the Galapagos where this perpetual over-heating problem could be cured once and for all; certainly, the prospect of a three thousand-mile passage to Tahiti without an engine was not an attractive one. There were also the equatorial doldrums to consider which straddled much of the Galapagos Archipelago and where the absence of winds could becalm a vessel for days. Without a working engine, *Bella Mama* could – in a worst-case scenario – be adrift for days in such windless climes.

Another consideration was the tendency for delivery captains to feel they had failed in their mission if the contracted destination was not reached on time. This macho mentality -- encouraged by Lavinia's exhortations to make up lost time – could encourage the taking of unnecessary risks. With a wife and two kids back home in Florida, Ewan hoped The Swede would be prudent enough not to venture beyond these islands without a proper functioning engine.

On the sailing front, meanwhile, the winds were favourable although it turned quite cold as they approached the Galapagos and its equatorial environs.

The cold waters of the Humboldt Current were the main reason for this chill factor which could also generate large patches of dense fog. The yacht's various manuals and charts warned of strong currents around the archipelago which could prove to be one of the more daunting challenges when approaching Academy Bay – notably for a vessel without engine power – should the wind fail. One solution might be to launch the dinghy and raft it onto *Bella Mama*'s port or starboard hull for use as a source of supplementary outboard engine power. For the moment, however, such considerations were still a hundred miles away.

When he took the helm at six o'clock next morning -- just in time for another splendid sunrise -- the GPS indicated they were 108 miles from Academy Bay. The chart positioned them at only half a minute of latitude from the equator. But so far, it seemed, no ceremonies were planned for crossing the line. King Neptune could sleep in peace.

Pierre made breakfast and served coffee, toast and cheese in the cockpit. Ove cleaned his teeth over the stern. About fifty yards behind him, a small school of what they took to be bottlenose whales tracked their wake for a short while and then disappeared. They had blunt and rounded heads and were slightly bigger than dolphins.

At which point Ewan asked The Swede for permission to use the satellite telephone and make a call to Jojo. The line was exceptionally clear and the call, as it turned out, somewhat timely. Back in England, his sister and husband were visiting Jojo and had just returned from taking her to hospital after the horse she'd been exercising trampled her ankle. She was now on crutches, they reported, and her leg had been x-rayed but, fortunately, there was no serious damage other than extensive bruising. Worse still, though, was the news that they had recently sold their *belle maison* in southwest France. After four years refurbishing, redecorating and making this lovely little village house habitable, they'd accepted an offer from a passing buyer. Ewan was stunned at the news...even in mid-Pacific.

It seemed so long since they'd last seen land that the anticipation of sighting the first of the Galapagos islands was immense. *Bella Mama* was now making good headway under sail and approaching the archipelago from the northeast but with her engine problem still unresolved. Then the small islet of Genovesa appeared on the horizon which was the first proof they had of reaching this most celebrated of Pacific island destinations. From their two-mile offshore vantage point, Genovesa appeared brown, arid, flat and not particularly inviting. They passed it on their starboard side and continued on the same course towards their destination -- Academy Bay at Puerto Ayora -- situated on the southern coast of Isla de Santa Cruz and still about eighty nautical miles away.

A few hours after sunset, at precisely eleven o'clock on June twenty-six, they crossed the equatorial meridian which bisects the Galapagos Archipelago and moved into planet earth's southern hemisphere. Ewan's mind wandered back to other more memorable crossings: as a boy on the way to and from Ceylon in the nineteen-fifties and then on a troopship as a young virgin soldier bound for Hong Kong in 1957 and, two years later, back again to Liverpool. All those occasions had been on large ocean vessels where crossing the line was marked by all manner of traditional poolside rituals and fun. Similar activities, he vaguely recalled, had been planned by Skipper Tad of the Old Crew. His young friends from British Columbia had never crossed the equator by sea and he planned to do things in style with a gourmet dinner, fine wine and King Neptune's full rite of passage. But Ewan reminded himself that the old order had included young romantics in love with life and thrilled at the prospect of an odyssey across the world's greatest ocean. He just happened to have the good fortune to fall into their midst and enjoy the vicarious thrill of being young again. How sad that it should all have ended in such bitterness and tears.

Now it was all quite different with not even a glass raised to toast the crossing. They were sailing by Swedish Rules…and Ove was below deck on his bunk worrying about a night arrival under sail without the benefits of a working engine. And what was more troubling: he had Lavinia on board to keep an eye on things. As if this weren't enough, the wind disappeared at three thirty hours and they were totally becalmed. The boat drifted for several hours out of sight of land into another magnificent dawn and then, as if by the throw of some celestial switch, a zephyr returned and *Bella Mama* was on her way again: her sails filling and her bow knifing through the deep blue waters of this unique location.

They tacked along the eastern coast of Santa Cruz for most of the day towards Academy Bay, the surrounding waters teeming with marine life. The island was a classic mid-Pacific volcano with black rocky coastal cliffs and a rounded rather than conical hinterland overlaid by luxuriant green vegetation, its uplands shrouded in cotton-wool clouds.

Their course took them inside an outcrop of offshore rocks where they narrowly missed hitting a giant turtle and, shortly afterwards, looked down in amazement at the aeronautical shape of a massive manta ray gliding by in the other direction. Then the sea turned blood red and they were reminded of nature's more brutal

161

moments…probably shark attacks on seals or dolphins. Overhead marauding gulls, albatrosses, terns and cormorants surveyed the carnage below and looked for scraps.

The next highlight that day was more sonic than visual: it occurred when – from below deck in the engine room – the skipper whooped like a demented Kentucky wrangler and emerged to proclaim a minor technological triumph: he had managed to dislodge the wretched impeller from the salt-water pump. A new one was inserted and, shortly afterwards, the engine started. The Yanmar whined contentedly and they breathed a sigh of relief; but, as so often in the past, their relief was short-lived. There was still no water coming from the exhaust which meant, *ipso facto*, there was no water cooling the engine's innards or keeping the fridge-freezer cold. Ove cut the motor and they continued under sail towards Academy Bay. Was there no justice?

Some time later, Lavinia surfaced and made herself a breakfast of coffee, toast and cereal, which she ate in the saloon. No one had seen her for three days. She then disappeared back into her cabin and re-emerged a few minutes later with a small, wooden, varnished box.

'Anyone for chess?' she asked.

Ove and Pierre exchanged glances, felt anxious but said nothing.

'We used to play on ski holidays,' Ewan volunteered.

'God loves you, honey. Let's have a game.'

The board was unfolded above on the cockpit table and several games played with Lavinia introducing some interesting new rules. Her chess skills were minimal and, despite Ewan's worst efforts, it seemed impossible to lose to the old dragon. Having volunteered his services, however, he now had to suffer the consequences.

'How many games you won?' she asked.

'I think we're about evens.'

'Don't you lie to me, sir. I know you're good. But look out tomorrow. I want revenge. You'll see. I'm not as bad as you think.'

The remarks seemed light-hearted so he assumed no damage had been done to the relationship. But his heart sank at the prospect of a daily tournament which he was unable to lose and which might gradually become a source of aggravation to this prickly adversary. It was important to remain in the old girl's good books if only to be sure of being paid and getting an air ticket home when they reached Tahiti.

It was well after dark when they sailed into Academy Bay and groped their way forward to the Puerto Ayora anchorage. Ove lowered the mainsail and used the Genoa and light airs to propel *Bella Mama* through the water in lieu of an ailing engine. Ewan was on the helm and when the GPS indicated four degrees and five minutes south he turned the bow westwards and made for the lights ahead. The anticipation and excitement at reaching their first landfall in the Galapagos was palpable.

Half an hour later, they dropped anchor and peered into the darkness to discern who their neighbours might be. These seemed to comprise a motley fleet of small freighters and fishing smacks, a large square-rigged clipper, a research vessel, a save-the-whale protection ship, numerous tour and dive boats and an assortment of private sailboats of varying dimensions and configurations. But the anticipation of seeing more of their surroundings in this eagerly-awaited destination was frustrated – as is so often the case – by a night time arrival.

Twenty-three

They woke to a bright, sunny day and found themselves in a far less developed port than the previous night's illuminations had suggested. In fact, there really were no docking facilities and so – along with an assortment of other vessels – they stayed at the Academy Bay anchorage and rowed the dinghy ashore. Lavinia assumed command and led her captain and crew to the local police and immigration post to arrange the appropriate inbound clearance. After a short delay, they were ushered into a large office where the island's *Comandante* sat behind an imposing desk thumbing through their passports. Outside in the courtyard, a line of uniformed militiamen were being inspected by an officer. Galapagos is a province of Ecuador and their uniforms reflected this sovereignty.

'*¿El barco tiene papeles?*' inquired *El Comandante* somewhat brusquely.

'He wants the boat's documentation,' Ewan interpreted.

'Ove, give the gentleman *Bella Mama*'s ownership and registration papers,' instructed Lavinia.

'*¿Quien es el proprietario?*' asked *El Comandante*.

'This lady is the boat's owner,' he replied.

'*Muy bien. Entonces, el barco y la proprietaria son de los Estatdos Unidos. ¿Es esto?*

'*Eso es,*' he confirmed…the boat and its owner were from the United States.

'*¿Y de donde salen los tripulantes?*'

Ewan explained that the crew were from Canada, Britain and Sweden. At which point the inquisition ended as the phone on *El Comandante*'s desk rang and a lengthy conversation ensued. A government delegation was arriving in two days' time from Quito, it seemed, and would include representatives from the

World Bank. Diplomatic passports were involved and the bearers had to be accorded the correct protocols. He hung up the phone and resumed his interrogation.

'¿Porque estan visitando Santa Cruz?'

'He wants to know why we're visiting Santa Cruz.'

'Tell him we've come to visit his beautiful island and to get supplies,' said the owner, 'and that we're on our way to Tahiti.'

He conveyed this to El Comandante in his best Spanish. El Comandante smiled warmly and said:

'Hablas bien el espanol.'

'Usted tambien,' said Ewan somewhat cheekily, hoping he got the joke.

El Comandante did and roared with laughter. He seemed satisfied that they were not drug traffickers, pirates, escaped convicts, whalers, prostitutes or smugglers and could be allowed to enter his fragile command. For the next half hour he delivered a lengthy lecture on the travel arrangements granted to visiting vessels like Bella Mama. Sailing permits were allowed to very few of the other Galapagos Islands, he explained.

At this point in the proceedings, Lavinia instructed Ewan to inform El Comandante that, in fact, she strongly disapproved of any form of tourism or inward migration to delicate ecological environments like the Galapagos and that the only reason for calling here at all was to replenish supplies and take on fuel. This meant that there was absolutely no question of desiring to visit any of the other islands within the archipelago.

'It can only cause further damage to a unique and vulnerable ecological site,' she added.

Suddenly, it seemed, their visit to these remote Pacific islands had been transformed from a voyage of discovery into a series of refuelling stops with little scope for exploration. Impressed at these modest aspirations, *El Comandante* stamped their passports and the interview was over. Ove returned to the docks in pursuit of cheap diesel and water pump impellers while Lavinia and Pierre wandered off to explore Puerto Aroya and find a restaurant for the evening's dinner which she'd promised to host.

To the west of the town were the offices of the Galapagos National Park and, beyond that, the Darwin Research Station. Ewan wandered along the shore front in that direction passing gift shops and small hotels with names like Hotel Sir Francis Drake, Posada Darwin and Hotel Castro. It was a pleasant hike and, once inside the wildlife sanctuary, viewing the giant tortoises and land iguanas protected within and learning of efforts to save them from extinction proved fascinating.

The legacy of Sir Charles Darwin's epic voyage to these islands in 1835 aboard *HMS Beagle* and its contribution to his theories on evolution attracted visitors from all over the world. To some of them, the question uppermost in their minds: was there a God or some supreme force overseeing our universe or were we merely biologically-evolved in a world devoid of divine spirit. To others, of course, the Galagagos was just another travel destination in the secular world of international tourism.

Already tourism was an important part of the local economy, attracting both Ecuadorians from the mainland and visitors from overseas. Managing this inward flow of outsiders and conserving the archipelago's unique bio-diversity, however, was a complicated balancing act between the forces of economic necessity and international conservation.

There were thirteen large and many small islands within the archipelago's high, rocky, volcanic protuberances which extended over an area of some three thousand square miles. The principal islands were Isabela (or Albemarle to the British), Fernandina (Narborough), Santiago, Santa Cruz (Indefatigable) and San Cristobal (Chatham). Discovered in 1535 by Tomas de Berlanga, they were for many years a haven for buccaneers and whalers until settled from Ecuador in 1835. This was the same year Darwin arrived aboard *Beagle* and, later, wrote of the great land tortoise – or *galapago* in Spanish -- the iguana and other creatures he encountered during his historic visit. A century later during the Second World War, the islands were used by American armed forces in hostilities against Japan as signal and weather stations and, in 1959, were designated as a national park and wildlife refuge by the Ecuador government.

ONCE BACK at the landing, Ewan joined the skipper for a beer and lunch. Far from being interested in the town, Ove's focus was on finding a new pump impeller for the Yanmar. His initial search had not been successful, notably on the linguistic front. Two of the impellers had recently self-destructed due to a lack of water circulation and he now had to rely on finding the appropriate component somewhere in this oceanic oasis. Progress across the Pacific from here to French Polynesia without a working engine was not an option, said The Swede, which came as a relief to his crew. There had been an uneasy suspicion that he might – in some atavistic display of Viking bravado – venture into this great oceanic unknown without a working engine in an effort to impress his new clients.

After lunch, Ewan hailed a taxi and explained to the driver what they were looking for. Their search took them on a mini-tour of the back streets, garages and workshops of the town in a fruitless quest for the right impeller. Next, they tried various local boat operators but none seemed to have the exact size of Jabsco impeller their marine engine required.

According to a helpful mechanic at the last boat yard on their itinerary, they needed to find a certain Manuel Alvarez who had a big selection of impellers in his workshop stockroom and might be able to assist. But Manuel was doing work at his small farm in the country and wouldn't be back in Puerto Ayora for several days. The taxi driver said he knew the way to his *finca*, so off they headed into the wooded hills of Santa Cruz in search of Manuel and an impeller.

Before long, they were in the back of beyond enjoying fabulous vistas towards the port anchorage in the distance below. The vegetation was rich and dense and the rocky escarpments a deep volcanic black like those in Hawaii. When they finally drove down a narrow dirt road to Manuel's *finca*, it turned out to be a junk yard of rusting machinery overrun by chickens, donkeys, rabbits and assorted farm animals. They showed Manuel the crumbling remains of their impeller which he instantly recognised.

'*Creo que tengo uno. Pero abajo en mi casa.*'

'He probably has one,' Ewan translated, 'but it's in his house back in Ayora where we've just come from.'

Fortunately, he agreed to drive back to town where they met him two hours later. There were three possible impeller sizes in his store room – one as specified – but they offered to buy them all. The Swede was desperate. Manuel wanted two hundred dollars for his efforts – impellers cost about fifteen dollars in the US – but Ove bargained him down to a hundred dollars which he accepted. The deal closed, they parted on the best of terms.

'*Adios y buen viaje,*' shouted Manuel with a big smile as they left, '*y cuidado las ballenas.*' Whales, it seemed, were an occupational hazard for fishermen in those parts. They also had an occasional propensity for trying to mate with the smooth contours of sailing yachts on account of their speed, shape and keel; an experience definitely to be avoided, advised a Frenchman recently arrived from the whale-rich waters of the Marquesas.

One hour later, The Swede had installed the new impeller and they were back in business with raw water gushing from the transom exhaust and the Yanmar cool, calm and injected. Would it last, they wondered. The crew freshened up and rowed back to shore for dinner.

Later that night they found Pierre in a nearby disco which reverberated to the pulsating rhythms of Ecuadorian *salsa* and other Latin American music. After several beers, he revealed that he'd been touring the local whore houses – of which there appeared to be many – and fallen in love with a local hooker. Ove warned him of the dangers of such liaisons and the hazards of jumping ship in the middle of the Pacific Ocean. The whole notion of mid-Pacific bordellos on Darwin's hallowed archipelago seemed incongruous, thought Ewan. Pierre concurred but said he must return to the brothel where he'd left his precious Panama hat. He wasn't seen again until the following morning when he scrambled back on board *Bella Mama* off a passing launch.

All this delighted Lavinia who had now taken the young French Canadian firmly under her maternal wing and revelled in his bawdy tales. There was no detail of his lascivious adventures, it seemed, which he wouldn't share with this lusty granny. The idea of a testosterone-packed young *Quebecois* sewing his oats on Darwin's evolutionary test bed seemed to leave her in a state of senile hilarity. Being isolated on *Bella Mama* for the next six weeks with such a potent toy-boy was orgasmic even at her advanced stage of life. She couldn't wait to cast off – with or without an engine – and sail into the Pacific Ocean and all its prospects. Having primed and encouraged his carnal appetites, would she now lure him into her cosy state room, they wondered. Only time and Pierre's demanding sexual appetite would tell. And the less one knew about the whole disgusting idea, thought Ewan, the better.

FULLY RECOVERED from the previous night's excesses, Pierre accompanied Ewan on a scuba excursion to the nearby seal colony of Isla Llave. An outcrop of black rocks and sandy beaches a few miles out from the Darwin Anchorage, Isla Llave was inhabited by a multitude of these playful creatures on land and in the surrounding waters. After a short boat ride, they donned wet suits, flippers and masks, fell backwards off the boat and were immediately cavorting with man's best friend beneath the waves. It was an exhilarating experience as dozens of these seals circled round them in the clear waters while others tumbled down the polished rocks into the surging seas.

After an hour, they climbed back on board and headed for a cliff creek along the shore of the mainland where basking white sharks lurked. Pedro, their guide, assured them that they were harmless. But the murky waters and surging seas made it impossible to locate the whereabouts of these creatures which – despite their alleged timidity – Pierre and Ewan were happy to forego. Sharks were not on their preferred list of under-water confrontations, particularly invisible ones. But overall, this excursion was more of what Ewan had expected in Isla de Santa Cruz rather than the bawdy whorehouses and *salsa* clubs. Pierre, of course, disagreed.

Once back on shore, the focus shifted to finding

food and diesel. Their local agent, Ricardo, said they would not be able to buy fuel until the fortnightly bunkering vessel arrived from Ecuador on Monday. So they retired to their bunks for another choppy, uncomfortable night at anchorage.

Next morning, Ove and Pierre set off in the dinghy with jerry cans to see how much diesel they could elicit from the town's only fuel station. The result was a twenty-gallon allocation which, according to Ricardo, was unlikely to be exceeded due to the island's many trucks and buses which also needed fuel. The skipper's only option was a local stevedore who could usually be persuaded to siphon off additional diesel from the fuel barge when it arrived. They were clearly on questionable legal terrain if caught and had to delay their departure until the fuel barge arrived.

So Pierre vanished on another quest for his Panamanian *sombrero*. Ewan rose early and went searching for an early-morning bar where he could watch the final match of the World Cup. There was extreme interest in the event throughout the Galapagos, so it wasn't too difficult to find a friendly football screen.

Waiting for the fuel vessel to arrive from the mainland resulted in much hanging around both on *Bella Mama* and ashore. This meant, among other things, further opportunities for The Swede to display his erudition. There was absolutely no escaping the man, it seemed, even in port. So they settled down to a dreary monologue, largely revolving around his early career as a diamond polisher and cutter; followed by ten years in the States as an illegal immigrant delivering boats; and then another ten years as a US citizen doing the same thing. Long sea voyages on small vessels – exciting and adventurous as they might seem – could sometimes include enforced periods of captivity such as this, the *per diem* no doubt providing some form of compensation.

A degree of impatience was beginning to emerge about this adventure, one sensed. Ewan had committed to honour a contract "to the Tuamotu Archipelago in French Polynesia via the Panama Canal, Galapagos and Marquesas" as agreed with the previous captain. So it was important not to allow moments of tedium or petty irritation to undermine the excitement and completion of this wonderful travel package. In one's senior years, he reflected, the best philosophy was to stand aside and let younger egos play the leadership stakes; and equally, to acquiesce in the initiatives of others and suppress any burning desire to do things better...assuming that one could. In such situations, of course, there was always the risk of becoming less industrious and appearing aloof. So Ewan resolved to recount fewer anecdotes – despite his original role of "interpreter, interesting old fart and sailor" – and let others hold the stage.

Talking of which, Ewan noticed how Tad – the previous skipper – in addition to being starkly different in all manner of ways from his Nordic successor, kept the boat cleaner and more shipshape. Ove's sense of justice also differed. He now wanted the cook-of-the-day to wash up the dishes as well. His logic: if you made a mess preparing a meal you should clean up afterwards as a sort of punishment rather than sharing out an unpopular chore.

The Swede's style of captaincy was one where the only initiatives allowed were his and virtually all others – no matter how trifling – immediately over-ruled. Pierre -- out of earshot and in French – felt this was the type of situation where alter-egos like Ove's fed on themselves and grew ever more *insupportable* as time went on: wise words from a young head. God knows

172

what the future held.

THEIR FINAL day in the Galapagos was a mad scramble to obtain fuel and finish off the food shopping. Pierre and Lavinia had concentrated their efforts on the latter and successfully found good sources of vacuum-packed beef, fresh greens and additional dry goods. But obtaining diesel to fill the supplementary oil drums – over one hundred gallons in total – had been quite a challenge with cultural and linguistic hurdles frustrating the captain and his first mate. In the end, they bought most of their needs from the lighter men engaged in discharging fuel from the visiting fuel tanker. In recompense, Ove was niggardly and only paid them eighty-eight cents a gallon – the pump rate – for the risk and effort made in siphoning and ferrying this contraband to his dockside drums. The crew had mixed feelings about the whole episode but dutifully lashed the two Texaco drums back into position at the aft quarters of *Bella Mama*'s stern. Lavinia -- who disapproved of most things she saw in this part of the Galapagos – was discreetly shielded from these unsavoury details. As far as she knew, her captain had re-fuelled, paid up and driven away just like any other gas station in Illinois.

With a new impeller installed, her fuel tanks re-charged and her victuals refreshed, *Bella Mama* slipped anchor at sunset and sailed out of Puerto Ayora's Academy Bay into the blackness of night. Just before midnight, they picked up a gentle breeze from the south-east, hoisted her sails, shut down the engine and knifed through the waters on a beam reach past Isla Isabela -- the archipelago's largest island – as forty-nine foot sloops like *Bella Mama* were supposed to do. The Wicked Witch and her micro-universe were back in business.

173

IN TODAY'S busy world of delivery captains, dependence on the various forms of satellite communications has almost become the norm. That, at least, was the case with Ove, The Swede. No ship's log was kept nor, as previously observed, was much care taken about crew safety and other nautical disciplines, although a daily GPS position was religiously plotted on the chart. The over-riding consideration was to deliver the vessel to its contracted destination – Auckland in time for the America's Cup – and to hell with the boy-scout niceties of the weekend sailor. This rather cavalier sense of urgency partly stemmed from the owners' desire to make up for lost time incurred by the previous captain. The exception to this was the monitoring of engine hours which were fastidiously noted against nautical miles covered and fuel consumed.

In the training manuals of maritime excellence, such over-reliance on satellite communications was once discouraged as dangerous and lazy. But the United States Navy's decision to eliminate the need on its vessels for a bridge officer with celestial navigation skills had changed all that. This apparent down-grading of the sextant and stars by the world's largest and most technologically-advanced navy in favour of navigation by satellite suggested The Swede was probably on the right track. The world was gradually abandoning dependence on navigation by dead reckoning and heavenly bodies in favour of GPS and electronic reliability.

This point was further demonstrated by their satellite telephone system which functioned with remarkable clarity when first employed by Ove a few days after leaving Panama. He called his wife in Boca Raton to tell her that all was well. 'Just another routine delivery, honey,' although, later, he admitted this was his first venture into the Pacific Ocean. The satellite phone had been leased from a marine electronics firm in Fort Lauderdale and – while rarely used on their earlier passages from Florida to Panama – now assumed greater importance as they crossed the vastness of the Pacific.

Apart from personal calls, the sat-link could also be used to obtain weather information or, *in extremis*, to send distress alerts. Satellite-based systems were gradually replacing the old short-wave radio communications on recreational vessels like *Bella Mama*. In addition to a hefty tariff for leasing the handset, calls cost about one dollar a minute. The skipper said they could use the phone once a week to call friends and family and painstakingly recorded the duration of each connection made. Charges would be deducted from their pay cheque at the end of the voyage, he explained. Ewan had every intention of using this arrangement to maintain contact with Jojo and his two daughters, family and friends.

SATELLITE NAVIGATION

Knowing where you are has always been critical to survival at sea. Ever since mariners first pointed their sextants at the stars, navigation has been limited by the accuracy of the instruments being employed. But the emergence of the Global Positioning System – with its six loops each of four orbiting satellites – has vastly increased navigational accuracy on planet earth where its impact has been revolutionary. Until its introduction, mariners traditionally relied on positioning and navigation systems with inherent limitations in terms of accuracy, availability and coverage. GPS, on the other hand, was a worldwide resource freely provided by the American government which allowed a sailor with the appropriate receiver to determine his exact position with remarkable precision.

How it worked was based on a constellation of 24 solar-powered satellites 12,000 miles above the earth and moving at 7,000 miles per hour; a series of earth monitoring stations; and receivers on the ground that used the satellites as precise reference points to triangulate their position. By measuring the travel time of a signal transmitted from each satellite, a receiver on the ground could calculate its distance from that satellite. When recording the signals from at least four satellites, a GPS receiver could then determine its latitude, longitude, altitude and time. What used to be a complex science necessitating the expertise of a celestial navigator was now a matter of pressing a few buttons.

Originally, the GPS had its roots in Cold War defence applications and was developed by the United States to consolidate the various guidance and navigational needs of its armed forces and avoid wasteful over-lap and unnecessary diversification. Its origin stemmed from earlier WW2 electronic systems such as the Loran and Decca types which used terrestrial radio communications as navigational aids. In 1959, however, Transit -- the first satellite-based navigation system – was developed by the Johns Hopkins University for the US Navy's nuclear submarine service and formed the technological foundation for a future Global Positioning System. Using a constellation of five satellites, it provided a navigational fix approximately once every hour.

In 1963, the Aerospace Corporation investigated the feasibility of a space-based, three-dimensional concept for high-speed vehicles such as aircraft and missiles. Theoretically, it involved measuring the arrival times of radio signals transmitted from satellites whose positions were precisely known. This provided the distances to the known satellite positions which, in turn, indicated a user's position. Similar defence systems like Timation – also for the USN – and the US Army's Secor systems were subsequently consolidated under Navsec (Navigation Satellite Executive Committee) in 1968 to determine the best satellite configuration to pursue.

A protracted political debate culminated in a more unified strategy within the US Department of Defence when, in December 1973, a new entity called the Navstar GPS was given the tentative go-ahead to incorporate the best of all known satellite navigation concepts and technology. The configuration selected was that of 24 satellites placed in 12-hour inclined orbits, with Rockwell International contracted to manufacture the satellites. The next decade became one of experimentation, evaluation and system testing. An additional specification required the GPS to detect nuclear explosions anywhere in the world. On 14 July 1983, the first GPS satellite to carry the new Nuclear

177

Detonation Detection System was successfully launched.

The Pentagon – America's military headquarters -- now had a remarkable new strategic weapon in its Cold War arsenal. With it, US instruments of war – whether manned fighter aircraft, unmanned cruise missiles, inter-continental ballistic missiles, nuclear submarines, battle tanks or unmanned air vehicles – could reach enemy targets with extraordinary accuracy.

In September 1983, however, an event occurred that would totally alter the application and complexion of this highly secret technological break-through. A Korean Air Lines airliner travelling New York-Anchorage-Seoul drifted off course into sensitive Soviet air space near the Sakhalin Islands, north of Japan, and was shot down by a Russian Su-15 fighter. All 269 passengers and crew were killed in what was undoubtedly a barbaric attack on a defenceless civil aircraft. The Russians justified their action by insisting South Korea was equipping its civil airliners with US spy cameras and over-flying sensitive military positions.

After an intense spate of diplomatic activity, it was accepted that flight KAL 007 – the doomed Boeing 747 with many Korean, American and other nationalities on board – had probably drifted off course through pilot error. This could not have happened, declared the US Federal Aviation Administration, if the airliner had been equipped with GPS navigation aids. Some version of this top secret technology had to be made available for civil aviation use so as to avoid a repeat of this shocking event.

Inevitably, the Pentagon's defence chiefs baulked at sharing such vital technology at a time of heightened Cold War tension. It had been specifically developed for defence purposes and should remain so. Deadlock

178

between the civil and military camps was eventually broken on 16 September 1983 when, to his enormous credit, President Ronald Reagan – incumbent US commander in chief -- agreed to make a version of GPS available to civil aircraft at no cost.

Henceforth, the GPS programme would have two separate applications: one, defence and managed by the Department of Defence; and the other, civil and managed by the Department of Transport. As part of its new responsibility, the DoT would be responsible for establishing an office to process civil user needs for information, data and assistance. The software for separating the military uses of GPS would be embodied in something called Selective Availability (SA) which involved the provision of a two-tier level of precision. The superior capability went to the military; the "degraded" version to civilian users. Similarly, SA provided the US government with an access control mechanism should it decide to withdraw GPS coverage. But the SA aspect was deactivated in August 1990 during the Persian Gulf War owing to the limited three-dimensional coverage provided by the Navstar GPS satellites in orbit at the time. In July 1991, it was reactivated at the end of hostilities. Between 1990-91, however, GPS was used by Allied forces under combat conditions for the first time. Its role in Operation Desert Storm was the first successful tactical use of space-based technology within an operational setting.

On the civil side, surveying became the first commercial GPS market to develop. To compensate for the limited number of satellites available in the early development phase in 1984, surveyors introduced a number of accuracy enhancement techniques including differential GPS which would later be used for other civil applications. In August 1991, the US revised its export regulation so as to make a clear distinction between military and civil GPS receivers. Under these, military receivers were treated as munitions with strict export restrictions, while civilian receivers were designated general destination items and available for export without restrictions.

On September 1991 the Americans informed the International Civil Aviation Organisation – a United Nations agency -- that they would make their standard GPS available to the international community on a continuous, worldwide basis with no direct user charges for a minimum of ten years. It was a generous gesture that brought remarkable benefits to the world of navigation as new applications were innovated. This was followed in September 1992 by an offer to extend the 1991 arrangement for the foreseeable future and -- subject to available funding -- to provide a minimum six-year notice of termination of GPS operations.

On 8 December 1993 – after almost 35 years under development – the GPS became fully operational with 24 satellites in orbit capable of delivering the original promise to civil users of one-hundred-metre accuracy on a continuous basis throughout the world. In a letter to ICAO dated 16 March 1995, President Bill Clinton reaffirmed the US's commitment to provide GPS signals to the international civilian community of users.

So far the GPS has cost the US taxpayer over $15 billion in development and operating costs. Whether Washington continues to invest, maintain and operate this costly but increasingly essential global navigation network in times of economic recession remains to be seen. Certainly, the US defence aspect and dependency are unlikely to alter. But the day may come when American taxpayers want a more equable cost sharing through some form of user tariff.

There are also some nations which dislike dependence for such vital communications on a foreign power and, in some cases, are seeking alternative arrangements. For this reason, other sovereign systems such as Russia's Glonass, Europe's Galileo, China's Compass and India's Irnss are in varying stages of development.

But the only time-tested sat-nav system for a forty-nine foot sailing yacht crossing the Pacific on a stormy night was unquestionably the GPS. America might be bullying pathetic little Cuba and earning a few black marks in the process, thought Ewan, but, my God, its technology was magnificent. Sat-nav was less heroic than the polished telescopes, sextants and distance logs of yester-year but it was certainly safer. Russia had already discovered how difficult it was to keep its Glonass satellites aloft and free of ultra-violet damage. So the world of recreational sailing and delivery captains was going to remain GPS-reliant for many more years to come.

Twenty-four

The first watch after leaving Academy Bay ran from midnight to zero-three-hundred hours. The weather was chilly with varying but helpful winds. With three crew members rotating helm duties around the clock, Ewan's next stint was from nine o'clock to noon. A brisk fifteen-knot wind from the south-southeast pushed them through the water over biggish swells as the last of the Galapagos Islands receded into the mist. It was a bright, sunny day which they hoped would augur well for conditions from here to the Marquesas in French Polynesia. By nine-thirty on day one, the GPS told them they had covered 102 miles.

After ablutions, Ewan made a breakfast of cereal, chopped apple and milk. Things were calm and the skipper appeared to have matters under control. There was still no sign of Lavinia who usually put in her first cockpit appearance after ten o'clock. By eleven they were on a course of 240 degrees with winds of 17-18 knots making a steady speed over a rather disorganised swell from east to west on *Bella Mama*'s port beam.

Next morning at nine-thirty – day two -- they recorded their first twenty-four-hour timed distance of 201 miles. This was an encouraging pace if maintained and reflected the favourable winds -- now attributed to the Southeast Trades -- and which seldom let their speed fall below eight knots. The sea that morning was choppy with six to ten foot swells floating across their bows in lazy formation. Winds varied from fourteen to twenty-two knots punctuated by occasional rain squalls.

Pierre fried pork steaks and onions for lunch which was his staple offering when on galley duties. He said this was because the quality of meat was excellent, easy to prepare and gastronomically idiot-proof. That night Ewan made *chow fan* which was well received by all except Lavinia who protested at the use of soya sauce to which she was allergic. Instead she had a fried egg and boiled rice.

Later, she told them the books that she'd brought on board at Panama were mainly about psychiatry, psychoanalysis and psychology. She attributed her particular interest in these subjects to her Jewish father and Roman Catholic mother.

'They endowed me with a worrying legacy of right-wing extremism and mental paranoia,' she said. 'My father brewed alcohol for Al Capone during Prohibition and my German mother pumped me full of guilt and rules. But we don't choose our folks, do we?' Her crew nodded collectively and smiled.

At nine-thirty on day three, the GPS said they had covered 205 miles over the past twenty-four hours. The ocean was immense and monotonous but its constantly changing features altered and affected the boat accordingly. Despite problems with a delinquent lee cloth around his bunk, Ewan had a good night's sleep and planned to fix it after his next watch. They were less than one-third of the way to the Marquesas Archipelago and a persistent lack of sleep would not be good for body, mind or soul.

At the end of day four, they had travelled 187 miles and the boat was leaking. This meant the bilges needed to be pumped manually for part of each watch. The bow anchor locker, despite being taped to prevent ingress, was now taking in sea water. Conversely, the fresh water being produced when they activated the generator was fastidiously conserved.

There seemed to be an eternity of space and time in Oceania and this crossing was certainly a unique experience. There had been other long sea voyages in Ewan's life aboard ocean liners from Liverpool to Bermuda during the war and from New York to

Southampton on the *Queen Mary* after the war in 1946; then a long voyage from Southampton to Colombo and vice versa in the 1950s; and in 1957 on a troopship from Liverpool to Hong Kong and back home again in 1959; as well as various holiday cruises in Indonesia and the Mediterranean. But never, he reflected, was there a trans-Pacific crossing in a forty-nine foot, fin-keel sloop over a distance of so many miles. In contemplative mood, his mind wandered over this and a changing assortment of other thoughts and future plans. If there was a God up there, he thanked Him for the blessings of family, friends and an experience like this.

On the next twenty-four hour cycle, they covered a distance of 192 miles and seemed to be maintaining pace. He took a shower, shampooed what was left of his hair and – after shaving – emerged on deck groomed and perfumed in a clean tee-shirt and shorts. At sea, he never wore footwear in hot weather. Later, he did laundry in a bucket of salt water and hung it on a line rigged between the two back stays off the stern. The mood on board was convivial.

But at sea, the unexpected is never far away. Despite being warned against applying the electric winches too forcefully, the stubborn Swede tightened the Profurl mainsail's halyard excessively and told the crew not to question his judgment "even if I'm wrong." He was, of course, very wrong and, just as they were about to enjoy a chicken curry for dinner, the main halyard snapped with an explosion that shook *Bella Mama* from stem to stern and brought the mainsail tumbling down onto the deck. The Swede moved effortlessly into panic mode as he struggled to cope with flogging sails and lashing lines under the spreader lights.

'Leave this one to me,' he shouted. The crew dutifully obeyed.

The topping-lift and the spinnaker halyard were

eventually jury rigged and the mainsail hauled two-thirds up the mast where it filled – on a reduced scale and a beam reach – as they resumed their passage. It was obvious that the cable had snapped because of the brutal way the skipper handled the power winches. Tad, his predecessor, was much more cautious and meticulous over such matters.

Later, curry was served and appreciated. Lavinia emerged from her state room and, after a briefing on these recent developments, heaped copious praise on her captain's nautical skills.

'God loves you, honey,' she cackled, 'you're one mighty fine captain.'

They sailed on into the night. The clocks were put back an hour as they crossed another fifteen-degree time zone on the westward passage. They had expected the climate at these equatorial latitudes to be hot and sultry. It was anything but. The cold Humboldt Current kept the southern part of the Galapagos Archipelago quite chilly, which it remained for some time on their passage towards the Marquesas. On helm duty at night, this called for cold weather gear.

DESPITE the previous day's rigging debacle, they continued to maintain a steady pace, covering 198 miles on day six. A spare halyard had been installed and the sails were back to full efficiency. But the wind slackened from twenty to fifteen knots, which was certain to reduce the distance travelled over the next twenty-four hours.

Meanwhile, Pierre told Ewan that – on a late-night visit to Lavinia's cabin – he'd been assured of a crew position as far as New Zealand. The plan now, it seemed, was to get *Bella Mama* to Auckland, where she'd be stored until New Year. However, weather windows – or a lack of them – might involve a protracted stopover in Tahiti. Ewan had been warming to Pierre and was delighted he was getting a paid crew slot (and God knows what else) all the way to the Antipodes. Pierre's focus was now on New Zealand, a country about which he seemed to know precious little. So Ewan filled in a few blanks and encouraged him to travel while young. He'd just turned twenty-five.

Later that day, at about a thousand miles from the Galapagos, this remote oceanic world they now inhabited was suddenly transformed by a remarkable maritime spectacle. Quite suddenly, without any forewarning, they were surrounded on all sides by hundreds of migrating dolphins for as far as the eye could see. Totally ignoring their presence – which was unusual for these inquisitive mammals – they moved purposefully across the ocean, cavorting and arcing into the sky, then disappearing beneath the waves. The impact of this performance was extraordinary. Whatever motivated them, the sight of such orchestrated energy was so unexpected and uplifting that nobody on *Bella Mama* had the presence of mind to grab a camera and photograph the event. Then, almost as quickly as the performance had begun, these lovely creatures were gone and the ocean had resumed its desultory complexion. It had been a timely reminder that, empty as the seas appeared on the surface, beneath the waves lurked another universe.

The Southeast Trade Winds continued to drive them effortlessly across the ocean. Having set the sails at Isla de Santa Cruz, they had not once needed to tack over the past seven days and, apart from the halyard incident, progress suggested a swift passage to Tahiti with only marginal course alterations required. But on day seven – after notching up 157 miles over the preceding twenty-four hour period – the wind dropped to light airs and the skipper decided to motor-sail so as to maintain momentum. For how long this would be necessary was unclear. They were still only one-third of the way to the Marquesas. Could this be the windless doldrums they'd so fortunately avoided when crossing the equator at the Galapagos?

Thereafter, life on *Bella Mama* boiled down to a tedious pattern of watches, sleep, ablutions, chess, books…and private thoughts. These turned to his daughter in Houston who, on the satellite phone yesterday, revealed that she had broken up with her boyfriend. He wondered if her mother's conversion to self-assertiveness and psychoanalysis was rubbing off and causing problems. He hoped not. These feminist traits could become over bearing and destructive. He called Jojo in England who told him the latest news on the home front: a Royal Navy frigate was slowly sinking somewhere in Australia after hitting a submerged rock. It was the summer silly season when Britain's newspapers – starved of news on the home front – hoped for another *Titanic* sea disaster or missing yacht drama to boost circulation and keep the presses rolling.

The wind gods had obviously taken exception to Ewan's theories about the Southeast Trades driving yachts effortlessly across a mighty ocean. After a brief overnight recovery, the breeze faded and the Yanmar was once again put to work. The apparent wind speed was now only nine knots.

He made a Spanish omelette for dinner along with a chopped onion and tomato salad. No complaints from the ship's complement this time. It had been a rather uneventful day dogged by less-than-usual progress and, in his current mood, anything that extended this passage for longer than necessary was unwelcome. Next morning, the skipper slowed the boat down and Pierre took a dip behind *Bella Mama,* towed on a long line and fender. The remainder of the crew kept a sharp look-out for marauding sharks and other undesirable predators that might devour their youthful helmsman and render them critically short-handed. Not that loss of a crew member would inconvenience The Swede who did most of the unscheduled tasks himself anyway…thus leaving his crew more time for reading, writing and dreaming up a greater variety of meals.

Lavinia, true to form, heaped praises and compliments on everyone and everything and currently seemed very satisfied with her crew and its mix of personalities. About herself, though, she was less flattering:

'I'm just a good old redneck by background,' she bellowed, a description occasionally illustrated by earthy curses and profane expletives.

But at seventy-nine years of age, one had to give her full marks for embarking on such lengthy voyages – for there had obviously been several others – even if she contributed little else but money and conversation to the proceedings. Lavinia wanted everything 'just to happen' and quite clearly regarded these voyages as an escape from the tedium of a humdrum home life. Back in Illinois, her husband's high-tech business boutique concentrated on manufacturing strategic materials for American weapon systems like the Patriot Missile. He was quite happy to finance his wife's appetite for boats and their crews. For who knows, one day she might not return.

'I'm quite certain Tom couldn't give a shit whether I live or die,' she guffawed one night over dinner and a third glass of wine. 'It's the perfect marriage: I circumnavigate the globe and he goes to hounds and charms the ladies.'

For a moment, Ewan felt a twinge of sympathy for The Wicked Witch but then thought better of it.

THE ENGINE HAD now been running non-stop for seventy-seven hours and, according to calculations, they'd travelled 105 nautical miles over the past twenty-four hours. It was day ten since the Galapagos and progress had been greatly reduced, adding appreciably to the bouts of boredom they all occasionally suffered. The vessel's total diesel capacity of 320 gallons generated a similar number of engine hours. So far they had consumed seventy-seven gallons, leaving another 243 operating hours or just over ten days. They definitely needed some wind. On the bonus side, they were still manually pumping the bilges, although there was now less intake of water to cope with. They also continued to produce fresh water at a rate of about forty gallons an hour with their Village Marine Tech reverse osmosis water-maker. This was powered by the boat's generator and did an excellent job for as long as it worked. As the unit was located in Ewan's tiny cabin, he usually knew when the captain was replenishing supplies to the main forward feed tank.

The sky was now pale-blue from horizon to horizon with the ocean over which they glided a wide, steel-blue expanse bulging under gentle swells. The skipper tidied lines, Lavinia reminisced, Pierre rested and Ewan wrote his journal. Earlier, they had emptied the eight jerry cans of diesel strapped along the forward decks into the main tank -- forty-two gallons in total; they had sailed 2,500 miles from Panama and were now two thousand miles from Tahiti. There was still no wind and – coincidentally – no mention had been made of the Marquesas.

Then, at around seventeen hundred hours, a light breeze filled the sails and allowed them to shut down the engine. Pierre made a dinner of fried steak, mashed potatoes, fried onions and tomato salad which went down well. Food had an amazing capacity to revive the flagging spirits...especially when washed down with a glass of *vin rouge*. Lavinia retired at six-thirty and Ewan resumed helm duty until nine o'clock. The sun set against a cloudless sky and they sailed on into the night at about five knots an hour.

Next day Ewan asked the skipper if he planned to sail directly to Tahiti or whether they would be arcing northwards to include the Marquesas on their route.

'Let's make that decision when we get to the waypoint,' he replied.

The next waypoint was about ninety miles from their present position so a decision would be forthcoming within the next twenty-four hours. Whether the owner had been consulted on this matter remained unclear; Ove was not particularly forthcoming about such matters. Next day, however, it emerged that they would bypass this remote group of islands which Lavinia decreed was "of no particular interest."

The Marquesas is one of the five archipelagos that constitute French Polynesia; the others being the Society Islands, Austral, Tuamotu and Gambier. But the present emphasis was on getting *Bella Mama* to Tahiti and then New Zealand. This was disappointing news but Lavinia and The Swede had an agenda and the crew were paid to follow orders. It meant another two weeks at sea to complete the remaining 1,800 miles to Papeete, the French territory's principal port. Ewan resolved to spend a week exploring Tahiti and the neighbouring islands before flying back to Fort Lauderdale and London. This would compensate in part for not visiting the Marquesas.

Later that day, the Southeast Trades returned and they were soon making a steady seven knots on a bearing of 244 degrees. Next morning, Lavinia emerged from below deck looking, to all intents and purposes, like the caricature of a grand old Mid-Western matron on her private yacht somewhere in the Pacific Ocean...which, of course, was precisely what she was. Ewan played chess with her and won two of three matches.

'God loves you, honey, you're a genius.'

She was getting better at the game since being encouraged to play in a bolder and more assertive manner. Pierre should have kept his mouth shut.

It seemed regrettable that they were not including the Marquesas in this trans-Pacific odyssey but, on the other hand, a prolonged passage could become wearisome. At times, they seemed to be ditching great chunks of time. Then he reminded himself of the unique circumstances of this voyage and – not for the first time -- revised his thinking. But after almost a year overseas, he was keen to get back to the UK and his life with Jojo...and, on the way, to see how *Contigo* was faring in Florida.

ON DAY FOURTEEN they travelled 147 nautical miles and encountered several maintenance problems. The water-maker was under-performing and the big hydraulic Autohelm 7000 had been shut down in favour of its busy little sister, the Autohelm 4000, which – despite its weaker belt-driven piloting muscle -- seemed far more dependable. Without an adequate supply of fresh water, they now washed the dishes with salt water plucked from the ocean in buckets and took their daily body bath in similar fashion at the back of the boat. They were making 5.2 knots on a course of 249 degrees and were still 991 miles from the next waypoint.

At this juncture in their trans-oceanic odyssey, they were surrounded on all sides by multitudes of flying fish which seemed to emerge from the crest of waves, glide effortlessly through the air for about fifty yards and then disappear back into the sea. On some mornings, several specimens would end up on the forward deck having failed, said Pierre in jocular mood, to see *Bella Mama*'s navigation lights.

On that particular day cockpit conversation revolved mainly around the subject of psychiatry and analysis. Lavinia told Ove that she'd always been a manic depressive and was often in therapy. All of her family – parents, siblings and children – were the same, she added. Like Ewan's ex-wife and sister-in-law, Lavinia devoured books about self-analysis, self-esteem and psychiatry -- usually written on the back of some doctoral research programme -- in considerable numbers. He remained sceptical about this aspect of American publishing and the quack science that kept it going, not to mention the damage it often inflicted on family cohesion. But on this occasion, he kept his own counsel. Too many Americans, from his experience, squandered hard-earned dollars confessing their emotional immaturity to these tight-lipped predators with their mood music and cosy clinics. The Swede revealed that he, too, had participated in group therapy sessions back in Florida and occasionally been sucked into this psycho-quagmire, which came as no surprise to Ewan. All these revelations, he reflected, had made for an above-average day aboard the good ship *Bella Mama*.

Next day was above-average for different reasons.

'Whales,' cried the captain. In a dramatic change of mood, they were surrounded by three Orca whales and braced themselves for a touch. Their giant forms broke the surface with blow holes spraying water into the air. As their white bellies passed under *Bella Mama*'s bows, Ewan wondered if this was a mating posture or if they preferred observing surface visitors from a comfortable upside-down posture. Either way, it was both exciting and terrifying. Two of the giants passed diagonally under *Bella Mama* several times while the bigger male provided a starboard escort about fifty feet away. The whole experience became increasingly alarming. Whales do occasionally collide and sink small vessels. And since they were far from land (four hundred miles north of Pitcairn Island to be precise) this was a worrying possibility. But after escorting them for half an hour, these three giants of the sea disappeared almost as quickly as they'd appeared.

'Either they're developing a battle plan,' said Ove, 'or we're too boring for further attention.'

It was impossible to encounter these creatures of the deep after so many days at sea and not to be profoundly moved by their presence, by their size and by their very existence. Not for the first time, he was overcome by a wave of emotion at the sheer satisfaction of being where he was. All this could, of course, be observed on television or read in books, but the reality of being in a remote part of the Pacific Ocean encountering a pod of whales was magnificent to experience. Some things in life were worth experiencing in reality rather than through the vicarious skills of the television screen and its craftsmen.

That night he celebrated the occasion by making a beef curry and – because her Mid-Western stomach was not attuned to spicy food -- frying a steak for Lavinia, all of which went down well. Somewhat selfishly, Ewan was volunteering for more than his share of galley duties to avoid the awful gastronomic concoctions of his companions. The danger of such altruism, of course, was being taken too much for granted as the ship's cook, particularly since the skipper had decreed there was no need for a galley roster. While all other tasks were shared out on a fairly democratic basis, the critical cooking duties – at which Ove was useless – were not. Unfair, cried a petty-minded inner voice. Such were the mental trials and tribulations of the long-haul sailor, thought Ewan.

Twenty-five

A s dawn broke in the east, *Bella Mama* goose-winged down-wind with her mainsail to port and her spinnaker set on the starboard bow. She had purpose. It was Sunday and they were within hours of sighting land for the first time in three weeks. Surging before a twenty-knot wind, the sloop's sleek hull made eight knots over the ground and looked and felt magnificent. On this lonely passage across a colossal ocean, not a single vessel had been sighted since they left the Galapagos. Then one night came an unexpected exception: a flashing strobe in a sea of stars that was either an orbiting satellite or the daily Air Tahiti flight from Papeete to Los Angeles. Other than this: nothing. The sense of distance and isolation helped give the mind perspective: on land man had size and presence; at sea he was almost invisible.

Nightfall and an enormous canopy of stars filled the heavens against the blue-black of a moonlit sky; some of these celestial bodies twinkled and prompted Ewan to ask himself if they really were stars and planets or man-made satellites. The daunting magnitude of darkness – streaked by the occasional meteorite plummeting earthwards in a dazzling display of light – could steer the night watchman down avenues of wonderment, fear and uncertainty. Where did it all end, he asked, this infinity of space and time? Surely, some supreme force was steering the ship. Or was it all just an empty void filled with fire, diabolical gases and hunks of volcanic debris?

Some sort of explanation seemed a reasonable request and kept his mind busy. Like Christ in the desert, did a sailor in this oceanic wilderness have similar thoughts? And was that the root of the problem for modern man: a hunter-gatherer's mind so programmed to problems, solutions and survival that it invented answers. Was theology, in other words, just a fabrication of the human mind? In a secular world increasingly shaped by technological excellence and scientific discovery, was there an explanation beyond these parameters? Or was religious faith simply a matter of what made the individual contented and fulfilled? Either way, a long voyage at sea was the right setting to make one's choice; a very personal choice which, somewhat surprisingly, Ewan decided to make.

Bella Mama sailed on into another day oblivious to Ewan's spiritual epiphany. Conditions were by now much lumpier and overcast. Ove wrestled with big following seas to prevent the boat from broaching as they raced downwind. Then at 13.15 hours – almost unexpectedly -- Pierre sighted land. It was a significant milestone on this epic voyage of self-discovery. The land in question was the tiny inhabited atoll of Takahina – sixteen degrees south and 140 degrees, ten minutes west -- on the outer edges of the Tuamotu Archipelago. They passed close to the atoll's north side and searched the shoreline for an outrigger paddling in their direction bringing French-speaking Polynesian maidens...or perhaps a spear-toting cannibal eager to have them for dinner. Pierre's imagination and Gallic sense of humour ran riot. Having toured the bordellos of Isla Santa Cruz, he clearly had similar plans for Papeete.

Shortly after, they sailed between the atolls of Fakahina and Fangatau -- its neighbour to the west -- whose profile was low-lying and very green from the palm trees that fringed its lagoon. At the western end they spotted a house; the chart indicated that it was probably situated close to a channel of unknown depth leading into the calm waters of an inner lagoon. Without an accurate depth reading, however, it was too risky to venture into this sheltered sanctum in rough seas. So they raced on pursued by enormous breaking waves and a brisk twenty-knot wind. Delighted with these developments, Lavinia called her husband in Illinois on the satellite phone to report their progress.

'Honey, it's land ho,' she bellowed into the hefty Iridium instrument. 'We've just sighted our first Polynesian atoll. We're about four hundred and thirty miles from Papeete.'

Next day, as if to re-assert her authority, Lavinia decreed a moratorium on the use of fresh water for everything except cooking and drinking. The water-maker was under-performing and not keeping up with their needs. The main tank was empty and the four smaller ones needed to be rationed. The crew, meanwhile, were getting filthier by the hour. So Ewan stripped naked and dumped several buckets of sea water over himself at the stern end of the deck. Similar problems afflicted the heads, which were having difficulty processing some of nature's larger offerings. His solution – a somewhat disgusting one -- was to remove the obstinate faeces from the bowl with a handful of toilet paper and discreetly toss it overboard through the porthole.

Around noon, they passed between another two atolls on their westward passage: Nihiru to the south and Taenga to the north. After so long at sea, land of any kind was wonderfully inviting. Once past these landmarks, Ewan resumed his book on Italian humanism. Although interesting, its scholarly nature called for a more classical education than his. But how else to learn about fourteenth and fifteenth century renaissance man with his appetite for ancient Greek and Roman manuscripts and classical writings on rhetoric, politics, philosophy, poetry *et alia*?

Late that afternoon, they sighted Makemo and sailed

along its north coast searching for the lighthouse indicated on the chart which marked an entry channel. The atoll – one of the group's biggest -- was about forty miles long and, like others within the archipelago, low-lying and palm-fringed. Just before sunset they located the light and turned into the channel towards the inner lagoon. Ewan was ordered to put out a radio call in French on channel sixteen for arrival instructions. Detailed guidance on how to proceed after the transit marks led them to a comfortable mooring in calm waters close to four other intrepid sailboats.

They dropped anchor and tuned in to the mellifluous rhythms of Polynesian music and ukuleles on the local radio station. Like Pierre, Ewan was excited at the prospect of visiting this tiny strip of Oceania; this far-flung corner of *le monde francophone.* He'd studied for a while in Paris after being demobbed from the army which, among other things, had converted him from being a chauvinistic Brit to a pro-European Francophile.

NEXT MORNING, Lavinia was in one of her less pleasant moods spitting sarcasm and unpleasantness in all directions for no apparent reason. Her inner demons were at work, muttered Pierre. Understanding her volatile personality was not easy. But the others were all keen to explore this tiny outpost of French imperialism. After rowing ashore, they wandered along the dusty, unpaved streets of Makemo's tiny port and chatted *en français* with some of the locals. From a trio of these, Ewan learnt that the radio directions received the previous night had come from a French ketch recently arrived from the Marquesas. Apparently, it had sought refuge in Makemo in order to undertake a bottom and keel inspection after being hit twice by unfriendly whales. The charts warn mariners of such dangers in the Marquesas, indicating that it is an important breeding ground for these mighty mammals. After this experience, the ketch – manned by a French couple and their two small children -- had immediately fled to the Tuamotu islands and were now being assisted by an American diver from one of the other vessels. Miraculously, the ketch had not only survived the whale attacks but had done so unscathed.

There were several small shops dotted around the tiny port but all seemed emphatically shut. Only the atoll's *boulangerie* was open, explained a diminutive old lady with shocking white hair and a walnut complexion. Her lined face was beautiful, thought Ewan.

'C'est le Quatorze Juillet, monsieur. Tout le monde est parti pour le festival des sports.'

It was Bastille Day and many of the 580 inhabitants of Makemo had left several days earlier to attend the Tuamotu inter-island sports celebrations on a neighbouring atoll. It was the biggest event of the year and extended over two weeks, she said. In addition to all the civic ceremonies and lusty renderings of *La Marseillaise*, it was an important opportunity for young islanders to find sweethearts and future spouses. Only the elderly folk – who'd seen it all before – were left behind to look after the island. She gave Ewan directions to the bakery and insisted they try the croissants – *'meilleurs qu'à Paris,'* she laughed -- apologising for the fact that they only baked bread once a day during festivities

The most prominent landmark in Makemo's low-profile skyline was a giant satellite dish which, in addition to providing this remote oceanic community with telephone and radio communications, beamed in live television news and programmes from Paris. It loomed over the other disparate bungalows, shacks and the gleaming white church like some uninvited contraption from outer space. Most of the many island communities within the five archipelagos of French Polynesia were similarly equipped, explained the barman at one of two cafes in the town centre.

'C'est comme nous étions aux Champs Elysées,' he laughed. *'On est bien servi, n'est-ce pas?'*

Ewan nodded and translated the barman's sense of contented metropolitan inclusiveness and followed Lavinia and flock up a dusty back street towards the little white church. It was set amidst curvaceous palm trees and a sandy cemetery of headstones – some wooden and others of white-washed stone -- and boasted a small bell mounted on its corrugated iron roof. Inside were neat rows of wooden pews over-hung by a dozen horizontal fans suspended from roof beams and presided over by a large ceramic Christ crucified in baroque style. Kneeling half-way up the nave was an elderly native woman with a shawl on her head fondling rosary beads and intoning Hail Marys. Lavinia walked up the aisle, genuflected at the altar and then crossed herself twice. The rest of *Bella Mama*'s team remained at the back of the church admiring its simplicity.

Once back at the dinghy, a debate suddenly flared up over the best route out to *Bella Mama,* which sat at anchor on a calm expanse of turquoise water in a veritable Pacific island paradise. Despite advice from all sides as to the safest course, The Swede's obdurate ego prevailed and he ploughed at full speed over a bed of coral heads that sheered off the outboard engine's propeller and cracked the dinghy's see-through bottom, before reaching the deeper water beyond. A stunned silence at this latest example of his pig-headedness was eventually broken by the owner.

'Gee captain that wasn't too smart. You'd better

check things out before we leave for Tahiti. Who knows, we might need the dinghy again.'

'Yes ma'm,' said The Swede somewhat sheepishly. Ewan hoped this might erode some of Lavinia's sycophantic enthusiasm for her captain and his questionable judgement. But then he back-tracked and thanked the gods for her decision to visit Makemo; at least this time, they were able to see something of out-island Polynesia. Bravo Lavinia, you cantankerous old bat, he muttered.

That night Ewan cooked a good *boeuf bourgingon* to celebrate the visit, adding copious amounts of red wine to the recipe to assure a gastronomic success. The meal -- which included a can of French *petit pois* and boiled potatoes – was well received by his companions and even elicited a minor commendation from Lavinia.

'God loves you, honey. This is one mighty fine beef stew you just cooked. I think it calls for another bottle of merlot, don't you Pierre?'

'Oui madame, tout de suite,' said the *Quebecois* as he vanished into Lavinia's state room in search of another bottle from her private cellar.

After dinner, they weighed anchor and made their way from the Makemo lagoon out through the channel to the open sea. It was another monochrome night flood-lit by a full moon. *Bella Mama* sailed in light airs over the flat waters, powered by her big, bosomy genoa. Ewan looked back at the atoll and glimpsed the satellite dish bathed in moonlight amidst a forest of palm fronds. It had been a brief but rewarding day that would stay with him for a long time. He wondered how many of Makemo's young men and women had found a soul mate at the inter-island games. This little community -- with its high-tech links to Mother France, its *boulangerie,* its little white chapel -- seemed so self-assured and confident of its place in the world: the very antithesis, thought Ewan, of the rootless mariner wandering the planet in search of self and home.

Twenty-six

After leaving Makemo that evening, *Bella Mama* sailed particularly well. She was, however, acquiring a long list of what aviation engineers sometimes refer to as deferred maintenance problems. These are repairs which do not prevent an aircraft being safely operated but have to be completed within a certain period of time to keep it that way. In *Bella Mama*'s case, the most pressing of these was a persistent ingress of water into her bilges. While there was no immediate risk of the vessel sinking or her sailing characteristics being in any way altered, the bilge pump's ability to keep pace with this intake occasionally moved into deficit. This meant some of the provisions stored under the cabin decking -- previously wrapped in newspaper to avoid perishing -- got soaked and began rotting. The Swede's general attitude to such matters was to postpone all non-essential repairs until the vessel's next port of call: Papeete.

That night Ewan took the Dog Watch and his mind quickly turned to planning the stopover in Tahiti where – assuming *Bella Mama* didn't founder over the next few days -- he would end his contract, as agreed, and leave the ship. A light breeze meant slower-than-usual progress, but a comfortable passage. They were now in French territorial waters which, in the case of her Polynesian sovereign assets, extended over some 2.5 million square kilometres. The ocean was enormous, with only the occasional sound of nocturnal birds migrating between atolls to interrupt the silence.

Once again, the tedium of a long-haul passage set Ewan's mind wandering in a multitude of directions: home, family, money, Tahiti. Time drifted by as *Bella Mama*'s working trio – Pierre, Ewan and The Swede –

divided three-hourly watches from one day to the next, their minds down-sized to a world of nights and days. Meanwhile, Lavinia – owner and *éminence grise* -- would, as usual, remain in her state room for days on end emerging only occasionally to forage for food before returning to her books. Her interest in playing chess or listening to Ove's hubristic anecdotes about his macho past or in the vessel's geographical progress seemed to have diminished. Ever since the Galapagos, the old lady had drifted out of everyone's focus – as sometimes happens to the elderly – only to re-emerge days later in full flow, re-invigorated and in high visual definition.

THE DIFFICULTY with her situation on board *Bella Mama* was that she lived outside the crew's rigid operating schedule of helm watches, meal preparations and rest periods. Had she been a more integral part of these activities rather than an eccentric old lady who liked to prepare her own food, read books and sleep, her absence would certainly have been noticed sooner. In the prevailing mood aboard this tiny universe, however, nobody was quite sure when last they'd seen her. Nor was anyone positively able to ascertain when or under what circumstances she might have disappeared.

The first inkling of her absence came when Pierre – her licentious toy-boy – emerged on deck one morning three days after leaving Makemo to report to Ove and Ewan that Lavinia was not in her cabin. Earlier, he'd knocked on the door of her state room, he explained, to ask if she would like a pre-breakfast cup of tea or coffee. As there was no response, Pierre assumed she was either asleep or in the shower and decided to try again later. On the second attempt he was still unable to summon a response. It was perhaps a measure of his cordial relations with Lavinia that, after a third unsuccessful attempt, he had the temerity to open her cabin door, something the others would not have dared to do. The queen-size bed, he said, was unmade and littered with items of clothing, books and envelopes and the door to the shower room ajar.

On a forty-nine foot vessel, searching for a missing member of crew should be a relatively simple task. However, Ewan and his companions undertook the task in the firm belief that Lavinia was still on board and part of their tiny world. It was, they later reflected, a complete denial of the possibility that – by whatever means – she was missing at sea. Ove began the first dragnet with a microscopic search of all aspects, nooks and crannies of *Bella Mama*'s topside decks and storage lockers for any evidence whatsoever of her presence. While he did so, Ewan put the boat on autopilot; and Pierre stood silently beside him in the cockpit.

Once The Swede had completed his topside search, the three men next undertook a minute search from stern to bow of the yacht's below-deck interior. All cabins, lockers and heads were searched for the slightest clue as to what might have befallen their owner. Scrutinising her comfortable state room with its queen-sized bed, well-upholstered chairs and spacious shower and toilet facilities was a necessary part of the procedure. But they now felt uncomfortable about invading the old lady's domain which was rapidly acquiring an eerie sense of unfolding tragedy.

The first sign of any on-board panic or reaction to these events occurred when Ove brought a shorthand pad from his cabin, sat at the salon table and began noting in worried detail when each member of the crew – himself included – had last seen Lavinia. The results were not reassuring. Ewan's last recollection of seeing her was as they left Makemo three days before. Pierre said his last sighting, he thought, was two days ago when he'd made her an afternoon cup of tea. The Swede said he thought he'd seen her outline at the galley sink two nights before.

As they gradually came to accept the notion of Lavinia's physical disappearance and the horror of her being left to drown in a vast ocean as her boat disappeared over the horizon, the question was what steps to take next.

'I think we'd better retrace our course and see if we can find her,' said The Swede. 'We'll do a reciprocal of our present course until sunset and then, if we fail to spot her, resume passage towards Tahiti. We'll make some course adjustments, of course, to offset wind and current leeway. This means I want all hands on deck scanning the sea with binoculars for a possible sighting. At the same time, I'll put out an urgent distress call on both the short-wave and VHF radios. Ewan, you'll repeat the whole process in French.'

'*Oui, mon capitain*,' replied Ewan in an effort to inject some levity into an increasingly grim scenario.

Ove disconnected the autopilot and swung the helm hard to port, bringing *Bella Mama* sharply through the eye of the wind and – after a cacophony of flogging sails – tightly hauling her onto a starboard tack. As the genoa and main sheets were winched in, the boat heeled to port and surged forward with a fresh burst of speed on a new course of 070 degrees. The engine was restarted and the two sources of propulsion quickly brought the vessel's GPS speed-over-ground to nine nautical miles. The roar of the wind and the white caps of breaking waves made it difficult to sight anything unusual in the surrounding seas. Both pairs of binoculars relentlessly swept the horizon towards the forward quarters as Ewan and Pierre scanned the seas.

Ewan felt an intense wave of nausea pass through his body at the thought of Lavinia being left alone to drown or be torn to pieces by marauding sharks in the vastness of the Pacific Ocean as *Bella Mama* sailed out of sight. But how could someone fall overboard unheard or unseen by other members of the crew? he wondered. Something wasn't quite right. Surely, a cry for help would have alerted someone. On the other hand, the background noise of the engines, the sea and the wind in the sails could easily have drowned out any call for help.

The captain's next move was to put out a May Day call on the shortwave and VHF radios reporting the loss of a crew member, the vessel's name and her present position and course. Ewan repeated the alert in French on both systems. This elicited an immediate response in English from a freighter located about fifty miles south of their position, heading for Tahiti, which requested additional information. Ove explained the old lady's mysterious disappearance and the assumption that she had probably fallen overboard some time during the last two or three days. He also advised them of his decision to retrace their route until nightfall, in the hope of finding some clue as to her fate and then resume passage to Papeete. The freighter's captain said he would relay this information to the French maritime authorities as well as any of the neighbouring atolls with whom he could make radio contact and also alert shipping in adjacent waters.

In an age of instant communications, Ewan wondered if it was appropriate at this point to call Lavinia's husband in Illinois on the satellite phone to inform him of her disappearance. He put the idea to The Swede who concurred with a despairing sigh, then handed him the bulky instrument and asked if he minded being the bearer of bad news.

Ewan took a deep breath, pressed the Tom Morgate dial button and waited for the familiar US ring tone to summon the old lady's old man.

'This is Tom Morgate,' came a chirpy voice down the line.

'Good evening Tom, this is Ewan on board *Bella Mama*.'

'Hi Ewan, nice to hear your voice. Lavinia tells me you're getting close to Tahiti. Have you arrived yet?'

'No, sir. In fact, we're actually sailing away from Tahiti at this very moment.'

'Why's that Ewan?'

'You see, it's about your wife, Tom.'

'What about my wife?'

'I'm afraid she's vanished,' said Ewan.

There was a long silence before Tom spoke again.

'What do you mean she's vanished?'

'About an hour ago, sir, we discovered that she was nowhere to be found on *Bella Mama*. We've searched every inch of the boat and are now back-tracking our course until nightfall to see if we can find her. Nobody remembers seeing her for at least two days. We've put out a May Day call and alerted vessels in the area to look out for her.'

'Good Lord what an ending. This is ridiculous. Did you look in her cabin? Is there anything unusual?'

'No Tom. Just a few books and clothes scattered on her bed.'

'Did nobody see her on deck or something? How can a person just disappear on a small craft without anyone noticing? Surely there's always somebody on the helm, right?'

'In theory: yes. But when the autopilot's in use, there are certainly times when the helm could be unmanned. And at night – it shouldn't happen, I know – a duty helmsman has been known to nod off.'

'Okay, I'll call you back shortly,' said Tom after another long pause, 'and tell Ove I want him on the line.'

The three survivors sat around the cockpit looking at each other. Ewan's imagination – fertile as ever – now began to wonder if any skulduggery by his shipmates could possibly explain The Wicked Witch's disappearance. He knew it wasn't him; but what about Pierre and Ove? What possible motive could they have? Surely not. But strange things happen at sea.

Then in the distance, for the first time since leaving Panama, came the distinctive whine of approaching turboprop aero-engines. The sound grew louder and signalled the appearance of a French Navy maritime patrol aircraft from the west. The big twin-engine Dassault-Breguet Atlantique roared past at about two hundred feet, wiggled its wings and then climbed away on a wide loop to the north. Ove seized the VHF microphone and called the aircraft on Channel 16 identifying the boat's name and repeating details of his earlier May Day alert.

'Roger that, captain,' said the aircraft's pilot in perfect English. 'Please switch to channel two-four.'

Ove changed channels on the boat's VHF and then explained that he had earlier altered course on a reciprocal of their original compass heading for Papeete in the hope of finding the lost crew member and would hold this course until nightfall. He also gave approximate details of *Bella Mama*'s bearing since leaving Makemo along with the relevant GPS coordinates and available compass readings. As the Frenchman methodically repeated each detail back to Ove, the Atlantique roared overhead for a second pass and then headed away towards Makemo at low altitude.

'We'll reconnoitre the passage from your current position to Makemo and hope to find the old lady,' said the pilot. '*Aurevoir et bonne chance*, captain. Over and out.'

Pierre muttered '*Vive la France*' in a burst of Gallic pride as the aircraft disappeared over the horizon. 'Those guys sound on the ball.'

'Indeed,' said Ewan. 'From memory, the Atlantique has a range of around five thousand miles and is probably the only maritime patrol aircraft between here and the US Coast Guard's Lockheed Orion operations in Panama. If Lavinia's still out there...they'll find her.'

In his heart of hearts, though, he knew the likelihood of finding her alive was diminishing by the hour. Nobody wore life jackets most of the time on *Bella Mama* -- least of all Lavinia or The Swede -- so she wouldn't survive for long. Perhaps that was her intention, he thought. Perhaps she simply wanted to bring her life to an end out there in the grim embrace of the vast Pacific. She'd already made many other ocean passages in the past with various hired skippers and crew and – uncharacteristically for a woman -- seemed curiously fascinated and attracted to sailing and the sea. Ewan remembered how the old lady had once said, shortly after leaving Panama, that if ever she died at sea, she would like to be buried at sea.

'Don't make no fuss over last rites, my darlings,' she said. 'Just heave me over the side and leave me to the sharks.'

At the time nobody thought much of this flippant remark. In retrospect, though, the words of its seventy-nine year-old author seemed to take on added meaning. Not many women of her vintage would fearlessly venture across oceans without giving some thought to their own mortality. After weeks of ploughing through a library of "psychological thrillers," thought Ewan, perhaps Lavinia just went mad one night and slipped inconspicuously overboard as part of a discreet euthanasia plan. No fuss. No hassle. No love.

As the sun set astern of *Bella Mama*, Ove plotted a new course, ordered Pierre to bring the vessel about and began retracing the route to Tahiti as agreed earlier in the day. Having found no sign of Lavinia, they now had to resume their onboard crewing duties almost as if nothing had happened. They sailed into a blazing sunset and, over the next hour, watched the sky gradually transform itself from a shocking celestial blue into a black, star-encrusted canopy.

Twenty-seven

The Atlantique reappeared the following morning and flew low overhead casting a long shadow on the sea. According to the pilot, there were no sightings on the previous day's search to Makemo and they were now making one final flight to the atoll on a slightly amended course in the hope of discovering some clue as to the fate of Lavinia. If this failed to produce any results, the search would be abandoned and the victim presumed lost at sea. Details of these flights and their results were being submitted to the Commissariat de la Police Nationale in Papeete, he said, to which Ove and all members of his crew must report immediately upon arrival.

After a sleepless night between watches, Ewan decided it was better not to engage in further discussions with Pierre or Ove about Lavinia's mysterious disappearance, in the belief that any investigation or questioning on the matter should be left to the police. This would make it easier for them to develop an objective picture of the circumstances surrounding her demise, based on individual interviews and to draw appropriate conclusions. If there were any question of malfeasance, he surmised, the police would know what to do.

But his suspicious mind continued to toy with a variety of scenarios in which each of his companions might want to murder The Wicked Witch. Even within the compact confines in which they'd lived since leaving Panama, he found it difficult to know exactly what kind of relationship each of his mates had developed with the owner. The French Canadian had certainly spent long periods with Lavinia in her state room. What transpired therein was a mystery upon which, uncharacteristically, the young man never expounded. Pierre had never been shy about recounting details of his amorous exploits whether on the beaches of Costa Rica or the brothels of Galapagos. Perhaps their time together was spent innocently discussing the virtues and demerits of psycho-analysis. Or perhaps he felt that having sex with a woman in her late seventies was not something worth bragging about.

The Swede, on the other hand, had been consistently lauded by Lavinia for his nautical skills and captaincy, even when these were manifestly wanting. After the costly debacle of the previous regime, however, Lavinia and her absentee husband were clearly relieved at any progress *Bella Mama* was making across the Pacific. Her support for everything Ove did or said was unwavering. He, too, had spent time with the old lady in the privacy of her state room, where Ewan assumed – perhaps erroneously – that he was keeping her informed of the vessel's progress towards Tahiti and making plans for the onward passage to New Zealand. He'd do all this, thought Ewan somewhat ungraciously, in that hideous Swedish-American drawl delivered with a slight curling of the upper left lip. The result was not pleasing to the ear but in the past it had probably eased The Swede's assimilation into redneck boating circles in Florida and elsewhere along the eastern seaboard when he was an illegal immigrant.

SHORTLY AFTER noon on Thursday, the beautiful island of Tahiti came soaring over the horizon in sharp focus and bold contrast. Its broad geological base and seven-thousand-foot Mount Orohena – shrouded in mist – filled their outlook with emerald green valleys that plunged down steep escarpments into dark-blue seas. On the east side of the island, along which they now sailed towards a distant headland, there seemed little sign of habitation. Ewan feasted his eyes on the black volcanic shoreline and marvelled at how an epic six-week delivery trip had turned into a four-month adventure and brought him to such spectacular places.

Bella Mama sped down wind at eight knots before a steady wind towards the island's most easterly point. *Pointe Venus*, an imposing lighthouse on the headland – Venetian in style and set amongst pine trees – signaled the next turning point, the last of Ewan's great odyssey. Although the chart indicated deep water close to the point, Ove decided to give it a wide berth. The shoreline and inland slopes were now becoming far more developed with imposing villas, hotels and small clusters of houses dotting the landscape as they sailed past.

Ewan made a quick scan of the local radio stations on his battered Radio Shack portable. It offered a cheerful medley of Franco-Polynesian culture: some in the vernacular, some in French, others in a mixed *patois* of both. The music was the same. Elsewhere, an English language bible channel from Hawaii declared to all who were listening that "every day is a gift to be cherished," a sentiment endorsed by Ewan with a nod. Pierre, however, roared with laughter.

'No sir, I've been on this goddamned boat too long. And every day on board is another day's fun wasted. I need female company. Captain Ove, can we please radio the port authorities and ask them to have four Polynesian beauties waiting for me on the dock when we arrive?'

'No Pierre, we can do no such thing,' said The Swede with Nordic solemnity, 'because first we have to explain to the Commissariat de la Police Nationale in Papeete what happened to Lavinia. Remember her?'

'Sorry skipper. Bad taste, I know. I'm just trying to inject a little humour into this voyage of the damned. And I'm so horny.'

It was an aspect of being young – this insatiable appetite for sexual gratification – that Ewan was glad to have outgrown. Some things definitely improved with age and maturity, he thought.

'I'm not interested in your sex life at the moment Pierre,' said The Swede. 'I'm more interested in getting this boat to Auckland or wherever Tom wants it to go now that Lavinia's out of the picture than who you're gonna screw in Tahiti.'

'Maybe you should call him and seek clarification,' interjected Ewan diplomatically. 'He said he wanted you on the phone next time we called. Would you like me to call him now?'

Ove nodded and waited as Ewan fetched the hefty handset and pressed the sat-phone autodial for Tom's number.

'Hello, it's Ewan here from *Bella Mama*. Can I speak to Mr Morgate please?'

No, said a stentorian female voice at the other end of the line. This was not possible because Tom had left for Tahiti the night before and might already be there.

'Thank you,' said Ewan. 'If he calls please tell him we're trying to make contact and will shortly arrive in Papeete at the city marina.'

Ewan pressed the disconnect button and returned the sat-phone to its cradle above the chart table. Two hours later they rounded a large freight terminal and naval base and motored across the bay towards the docking slips strung out in a wide arc along the tree-lined Boulevard Pomare. Standing on the promenade, close to an imposing monument to General de Gaulle, stood two tall men: one white-haired and elderly, the other dressed in khaki uniform and *kepi*. They pointed to an appropriate slip into which Ove skillfully reversed after first dropping *Bella Mama's* forward anchor.

'*Bonjour capitain,*' said the gendarme. '*Bienvenue à*

215

Papeete. Vous devez m'accompagner avec votre equipe à la Comissariat dans l'Avenue Bruat, s'il vous plait.'

Ewan translated the instructions to The Swede and then looked questioningly at the older man with the white hair.

'Hi, I'm Tom Morgate,' he said. 'You must be Ewan and this, I guess, is Ove. The young guy's Pierre, right?'

Ove confirmed the roll call and asked what documents were needed. The gendarme – now in English – said that passports and the vessel's documentation and log book would be required for identification purposes. First, though, he wished to board and inspect the yacht. Two other policemen appeared from behind a vehicle parked on Boulevard Pomare and prepared to board. Ove and his crew were to disembark before they began their work, he said.

After the inspection had been completed, the entire group turned left along Boulevard Pomare and then right onto Avenue Bruat and walked towards an imposing *fin de siècle* building with the words Palais de Justice boldly inscribed in gold lettering across the portal. The character and architecture of this part of administrative Papeete reminded Ewan of Toulouse and various other provincial prefectures in metropolitan France he had visited as a journalist.

Inside the police headquarters, they were led along vaulted corridors with splendid mahogany doors on either side to the office of one Inspecteur Francois Brunet and ushered into a large room adorned with portrait photographs of Jacques Chirac, Charles de Gaulle and Marshall Foch. Inspector Brunet explained that each member of the vessel's crew and Tom Morgate, as its owner, would be separately questioned by a panel of two police officers and a judge to determine the circumstances surrounding the disappearance of a US citizen by the name of Lavinia Morgate and to decide what further action, if any, needed to be taken.

The interviews would start in half an hour and each take about forty-five minutes. A written schedule was distributed pointing out that, once interrogated, individuals could under no circumstances discuss or have contact with those still pending interview and would be asked to leave the building by a different exit. All interviewees must report to Inspector Brunet's office punctually the next morning at ten o'clock, it ended.

Ewan's questioning by the investigating triumvirate turned out to be surprisingly bureaucratic and prosaic in its procedures. He had expected the rigour of the Napoleonic inquisitorial system to be relentless and imaginative in the hands of skilled prosecutors determined to solve the mystery of Lavinia Morgate's disappearance. In reality, he felt the entire process was a second-tier version of French jurisprudence. Because the circumstances involved the fate of a foreign national aboard a foreign vessel crewed by foreigners, it seemed that the case was of only marginal relevance to France and the administration of its *territoires d'outre-mer*. If one were part of the French universe, the full integrity and majesty of its legal system would apply and no effort be spared in finding the truth behind The Wicked Witch's fate. If one were not part of this Gallic club, Ewan reflected, then one had to make do with the mediocrity of its conclusions.

Next morning this was borne out by the judge who, with a slight pouting of the mouth and shaking of her head, said it was impossible to conclude other than that Lavinia Morgate "a US citizen from Illinois," had either fallen overboard and been the victim of a tragic accident or had taken her own life in a similar fashion.

All four protagonists in this drama, she said, had been independently interviewed and all had confirmed (a) Lavinia's actual presence on the vessel and the three crew members had (b) reiterated details of her mysterious disappearance in the waters somewhere between Makemo and Tahiti. In no case had there been any suggestion by any of the four individuals interviewed of foul play nor was there any evidence of violence against Lavinia detected by the gendarmes during their hour-long inspection of *Bella Mama* the previous day.

Consequently, no prosecution or further action was called for and they were free to collect their passports and the vessel documents and to continue their travel arrangements within French Polynesia or beyond. A full report of the inquest would be sent to the appropriate consular authorities at the American Embassy in Fiji which served French Polynesia. Her summary concluded, the judge rose, smiled expansively and left the chamber followed by the two officiating police officers.

As they left the building, Morgate took Ewan aside and invited him to dinner that evening at the Tahiti Sheraton where he was staying. The invitation provided a revealing insight into the unusual marital arrangements between this genial gentleman and his late wife Lavinia. She had, he explained, made at least three circumnavigations in similar circumstances aboard various vessels which he had sponsored over the years. They'd been manned by a motley assortment of professional captains -- Ukrainians, Russians, Italians, British, Irish -- and countless freelance crew recruited on the hoof and of varying competence. It had, he freely admitted, allowed him to lead a "more independent personal lifestyle" and her to find "God knows what pleasure with God knows whom wandering the seas and oceans of the world."

As a trained nurse, he added, she had a long history of involvement in local health care matters – particularly those relating to mental health – and sat on various state and community panels. In this respect, she had an insight into some of the less pleasant aspects of social life in a backward corner of America which probably explained her obsession with books on psychology and analysis.

'Southern Illinois is more Deep South than the rest of the state,' he added, 'especially the country folk. As a child raised on farms before the war and during Prohibition, she'd witnessed everything from negro lynchings to extra-judicial killings. And her father had made moonshine for Al Capone's gang up north in Chicago which wasn't uncommon in those parts.'

'What's an extra-judicial killing?' asked Ewan.

'Well, one story she often told happened in a small community near her daddy's holding and involved a guy who used to get drunk every night and beat his wife. Eventually, this farmer's neighbours had had enough of these battles and decided on a course of action. Next morning, as the guy stepped out on his way to work in the fields, a volley of gun shots rang out from the nearby houses killing him instantly. Later, the police reported he'd been hit fifteen times by bullets of varying caliber. No further action was taken. It's where rustic folk in under-policed communities take the law into their own hands. Sometimes it's pretty rough justice. But that's part of the history of America, I'm afraid.

'We fell out of love a long time ago,' said Morgate after a long pause, 'but we were never prepared – on either side – to renounce our longstanding relationship. Lavinia helped and supported me in all sorts of ways over many years to build up our business and family interests. Our success was a joint-venture in every sense of the word and I would never ever have traded her in for a younger model. I'm a wealthy man and that was always an option. But it would have been a disgusting act of betrayal and humiliation for her.'

After dinner, they retired to the Beachcomber Bar where, over several Hinano lagers, Tom gave Ewan his ticket on Air Tahiti back to Charles de Gaulle Airport in Paris.

'There's no direct flight to London, so this will have to do. And thanks again for staying with us this far. I'm sure it had its difficult moments.'

'A ticket to Paris seems an appropriate ending,' said Ewan as they rose to leave. 'Gauguin would have approved. I only wish it had ended less tragically. Not knowing what happened to Lavinia will be a difficult legacy for you and your family to live with. It will be for me, too. Some things in life are incomplete and stay that way.'

'I guess so,' said Tom as they strolled across the lobby. 'But we always knew something bad would happen to her. One way or another, life must end.' With that, he waved farewell, smiled painfully and vanished into the lift. It was the last Ewan ever saw of Tom Morgate.

Twenty-eight

The morning after dining with Tom Morgate, Ewan Marshbanks packed his rucksack, bade farewell to Ove and Pierre and disembarked from *Bella Mama* for the last time. He'd fulfilled his original contract with Tad to sail, to interpret, to cook and to crew on the Morgates' yacht from Fort Lauderdale to Papeete. It was time now to move on. He wanted to explore Tahiti and the neighbouring island of Moorea. Pristine rock pools, unspoilt rain forests, cascading waterfalls, giant ferns, exotic butterflies, birds of paradise and spectacular views: all beckoned.

First, though, he had to find somewhere to stay. He strode purposefully along Boulevard Pomare for a few hundred yards then, almost instinctively, turned to take a last lingering look at the sleek lines of the sailboat that had brought him so far across the Pacific. Here was a final photo. He raised the camera to his eye and framed *Bella Mama* and her skeleton crew -- still busily tending lines on the foredeck -- for a last memory frozen in time…and then continued on his way.

Papeete had all the trappings of a prosperous French seaside resort with an abundance of luxury hotels, auberges, pensions and youth hostels to meet all needs and budgets. Finding accommodation would present no difficulty. He'd already noted how expensive things were when checking rates at the Tahiti Tourism Office. The Hotel Reine Victoria was categorized in local tourism literature as *petite hotellerie familiale* and turned out to be an upstairs, city-centre establishment operated by a French Algerian called Bruno. It offered modest lodging in either dormitory digs or small air-conditioned rooms, he explained. Not succumbing to extravagance, Ewan opted for a dormitory in which -- as luck would have it – he turned out to be the sole

221

occupant. His many years working as a reporter in Asia had inured him to all types of accommodation, from luxurious five-star hotels to village huts with dirt floors.

Later that evening, after showering and shaving, he stuffed his valuables into a small backpack and set off to find a call box that he'd spotted earlier in the afternoon on Avenue Baurat to telephone a certain Vincent Bayol of Polynesian Hiking Tours. He was anxious to make travel plans for the next few days and figured the tour operator might still be in his office. As he left the Victoria, however, he saw that Bruno was dealing rather vocally and angrily with two unruly Tahitian drunks at the hotel entrance downstairs. He sidled past them avoiding involvement or eye contact.

When he found the phone booth and started making his call, Ewan noticed from the corner of his eye that the two burly drunks were now walking in his direction. They lingered close to the booth for a few minutes as if waiting to use the telephone. Then suddenly the larger of the two men lunged violently through the door and grabbed the phone card from the machine. As Ewan shouted in protest, the intruder withdrew, placed the card in his wallet with some deliberation and then laughed mockingly in his direction. As this happened, his companion grabbed the backpack at Ewan's feet below the kiosk's half-door and bolted across the road with his accomplice hot on his heels. When he realised what was happening, Ewan burst out of the kiosk and gave chase down a temporary pedestrian passageway constructed around the perimeter of a large building site. But both men had already disappeared. He stood for a moment shocked by what had happened with only the sound of a distant aircraft to break the awful silence.

Ewan Marshbanks – the international traveller, mariner, reporter, interpreter and street-wise nomad --

had been mugged in Tahiti by two local drunks employing the oldest diversionary tricks in the book. He had obviously been at sea for far too long. A little further along the passage, his rifled backpack lay in disarray on the ground. An old man walking his dog offered to help him search the abandoned building but with only a box of matches for illumination, it was to no avail. In just a matter of thirty seconds, he had lost his British passport, his US Green Card, his US Social Security Card, his Samsung camera, his air ticket to Paris and – most devastating of all – his Psion electronic organiser containing the contact details of over 750 friends, relatives and professional news sources around the world.

The old man pointed to the police headquarters in the distance – it was the same building Ewan had visited the day before -- and urged him to report the incident as soon as possible, which he did. Although sympathetic, the duty officers inspired little confidence and asked if he wanted to lodge an official complaint. This took an hour to complete and left Ewan unimpressed at their competence in either computer skills or law and order. Tahiti had a serious drug and crime problem, they explained, particularly among disaffected Polynesian youths living on French welfare benefits. Along with high costs, it was another reason why so few international tourists came to Tahiti these days, they laughed. Ewan was not amused at their casual flippancy but said nothing.

Later, the police lent him a torch to make a more thorough search of the neighbourhood where he'd been mugged in the hope of finding some of his stolen possessions. For the next few hours – until well after midnight – he scoured the unfamiliar streets and alleyways of central Papeete desperately searching in public waste bins, gutters, parks, bushes and building sites where the muggers might have dumped items considered of no value as they made their getaway. It was a hopeless task, he knew, but helped alleviate the burning rage that consumed his inner being.

The implications of the mugging to his travel plans were profound. Coming only weeks after the 9/11 attack on New York's World Trade Center and the Pentagon in Washington, the loss of his passport and US visa placed him in a particularly awkward position. Being stranded in mid-Pacific without travel documents was not an ideal situation at the best of times. French Polynesia might be the right place to be mugged if you were French, thought Ewan, but for a Brit with a US Green Card? Forget it. The severe tightening up of America's border controls and the massive shake-up of its homeland security systems meant there would certainly be long delays in replacing lost travel documents. And without them, he was marooned.

This was confirmed next morning when he reported the night's events to Marie-Claire, the charming lady who had issued his ticket to Tom at the offices of Air Tahiti the day before. Replacing an airline ticket was no problem, she explained, but boarding an aircraft without the necessary immigration papers was mission impossible in today's political climate.

The extraordinary images from New York of crumbling skyscrapers had transfixed and paralysed whole segments of the global transport system, notably that of aviation. The apparent vulnerability to such attacks and the complete impotence and inadequacy of the super-power's air defence systems had been a shocking wake-up call. There were absolutely no informal arrangements an airline could expect to make with US Customs and Immigration these days. And since Air Tahiti's flight to Paris made a stopover in Los Angeles, a solution had to be found before he could board the jet.

'Without a passport or a visa – and you can't get one without the other – the situation becomes very complicated indeed,' she said. 'Fortunately for you, though, there's a British consul in Papeete. *Il est tres gentil et va surement vous aider.* Also, Mr Morgate gave me a photocopy of your passport which will assist him, I am sure.'

Marie-Claire was desperately attractive, thought Ewan, but almost certainly married. She had that indefinable quality that had nothing to do with makeup, fashion or veneer but stemmed rather from primordial French femininity. A wedding ring on her left hand probably confirmed her marital status. She could, of course, be separated or divorced. His mind wandered.

'*Votre mari est militaire*? he asked casually.

'*Oui, il est pilote dans l'armee de l'air,*' she smiled with an intuitive glance.

'He's a lucky man.'

'You had better stop flirting with a married woman and find your consulate *toute de suite, monsieur,*' she instructed with a slight smile. 'Here's the address.'

Many of the overseas residents from metropolitan France had initially been brought to Tahiti on military service as part of General de Gaulle's post-war drive to develop an independent nuclear defence capability – the so-called *force de frappe* -- and some had retired there and taken advantage of various tax inducements to counter demands for independence from the indigenous population. Some of French Polynesia's more remote and uninhabited atolls served as useful nuclear and missile test sites for the development of these weapon systems and had brought substantial inward investment to French Polynesia in the process. Ewan wondered if Marie-Claire and her Air Force husband would follow the same path into *la retraite* –

that sacred component of French life -- but thought better of pursuing things further as his mind returned to more serious matters.

The British Consul turned out not to be British at all but an amiable New Zealander and longtime resident called Bob Weaver. He'd originally come to Papeete in 1966 as Air New Zealand's local manager, married a local Polynesian woman and, as part of the job, assumed the role of Her Majesty's Honorary British Consul. When he talked on the telephone, Weaver's command of French was a miracle of hybrid *franglais,* Kiwi syntax and good humour underpinned by a determined desire to communicate with the other party.

Having listened to Ewan's story – variations of which he'd heard many times before – Weaver offered three solutions to his predicament. The first was to fly to New Zealand via Auckland and obtain a new passport at the British High Commission in Wellington. The second was to contact the nearest US consulate in Fiji (about three thousand kilometres away) and see if they would replace his Green Card for entry to the States; recent experience of this option, said Weaver, had not been good since 9/11. The third option was to fly to Paris with Air Tahiti using an Emergency British Passport and then, once inside the European Union, proceed to London. He could help with the first and third options but not the second.

As Ewan already had a ticket to Paris, the third route home via France seemed the obvious choice. Before any temporary travel document could be issued, however, the consul needed clearance from the British High Commission in Wellington which might, in turn, require clearance from London. The fact that Ewan had obtained his stolen passport number from Marie-Claire and also possessed a suitable photo-identity, date of birth and address via an EU driving licence should make things easier, explained Weaver. Wellington was usually pretty fast in such cases but the upcoming weekend would add extra time.

Twenty-nine

Vincent Bayol listened attentively to Ewan's story that afternoon as he explained the mugging episode and the attendant travel complications, then suggested as an antidote to his disenchantment with Tahiti that he take a full-day hike across the nearby island of Moorea. He and his wife would be happy to add his name to their group for tomorrow's excursion which included two other visitors to the islands. Like Marie-Claire's husband, Vincent had come to Tahiti on military service and, after twenty years in the French Navy, taken local retirement and developed a lucrative and healthy lifestyle operating hikes around Moorea and Tahiti. According to Weaver, he possessed an encyclopedic knowledge of the local flora and fauna which added great quality and texture to his excursions.

Next morning, Ewan caught the catamaran ferry – *Eremeti IV* – from Papeete docks at eight o'clock, feasting his eyes on the scenic splendours of Moorea's soaring peaks and cliffs as the vessel sped towards the island's shoreline and coastal reefs. Once off the ferry, he soon located Vincent and his group and set off with them at a vigorous, sometimes arduous, pace up through abundant vegetation onto a mountain ridge with splendid views towards Cook Bay.

He could well understand why it was that so many local residents preferred to live in Moorea and commute each day by ferry to work in Tahiti. The coastal road was surrounded on either side by elegant homes and uncluttered residential areas and seemed wonderfully unspoilt and tranquil. After trekking inland towards a pierced mountain with a curious geological eye that framed images of the sea beyond, Vincent led his group over the ridge and down a dusty track into a wide crater dotted across its fertile base with small farms and palm groves. From there, after a very cold beer at the local café, it was a short walk back to the ferry.

Vincent picked him up again the following morning to join a larger group of hikers – all French except for one young Japanese woman -- for a more ambitious expedition into the misty valleys and mountains of Tahiti. Initially, they followed the course of a tortuous rocky river surrounded by dense vegetation and rain forests, taking the occasional break for a swim in lucid pools of cool water to sooth their aching limbs.

They were followed in these efforts by a tenacious village mongrel which wagged its tail continuously and seemed delighted at their presence. As the hikers scaled slippery rocks and clung to well-placed ropes with which to battle against the oncoming cascades of water, the dog – perhaps recognising its prehensile limitations – eventually decided to settle down on a rock and await their return.

As the ascent became more precipitous and demanding, Ewan marvelled at the dripping forests of giant ferns, brilliant butterflies, banana plants and palm fronds beyond which appeared hazy glimpses of distant shorelines and ocean waters through diaphanous veils of mist and sunshine. His long voyage across the Pacific to this sub-tropical paradise and the tawdry mugging of two nights ago would not have been complete or balanced – in a paradoxical and perverse sort of way -- without these treks into the uplands of Moorea and Tahiti.

But the mugging had added a sense of angst and urgency to his Polynesian travel plans; plans which he had so often contemplated during those long watches on the helm across the Pacific. The sense of being in a geopolitical limbo – a British subject stuck in a distant

French colony off an American yacht without travel documents only weeks after a dreadful terrorist attack on New York – now left him with a need to escape this awful jam.

The odyssey on *Bella Mama* had been a wonderful therapy for some of life's recent disappointments and sadness. Now, ironically, being stranded and mugged in Tahiti had backed him into another emotional impasse where he felt uncomfortable and reminded of things past that he wanted to forget. He knew, of course, that the mugging was only a temporary setback compared to some of the other challenges he had faced. But it still left him uneasy and aware of the fact that an Emergency Passport curtailed any scope for his forthcoming travel plans. It was a document issued for a specific journey with very little flexibility on dates or itinerary.

'Given the current international travel scenario, an expeditious timetable and routing would be your best bet and most advisable,' said Weaver. 'Trying to deviate from the travel arrangements documented on an Emergency Passport might get you into serious difficulties. The sooner you return to the UK and replace your passport and other documents the better. I've seen yachtsmen like yourself get into awful screw-ups with police and immigration on account of not having proper travel and vessel documentation.'

EWAN ROSE EARLY next morning and, after a light breakfast of *tartine beurré* dunked in c*afé au lait,* set off at a brisk pace for the Honorary British Consul's office. The weekend had gone well but his mind would not rest until he knew if Weaver had secured clearance from the British High Commission in Wellington to issue him an Emergency Passport back to London.

'Good news, old boy,' said Weaver as he entered his

office some time later. 'The okay's come through from New Zealand. Apparently there was no need to seek authority from London. So all I need now is sight of your airline ticket or travel itinerary and you'll have a valid travel document to get you home and on your way.'

Ewan handed him the ticket which, after close scrutiny, Weaver photocopied and carefully stapled to a companion document before filing both sheets in a large steel cabinet at the corner of his spacious office. He returned the Air Tahiti ticket to Ewan and gave him the Emergency British Passport -- a single sheet of A4 stationery over-printed with the royal coat of arms and his precise travel particulars -- bowing briefly as he did so. Ewan smiled at the satire, thanked him for his help, shook his hand warmly and departed.

Back at the Hotel Reine Victoria, he packed his rucksack, settled the account with Bruno and took a bus from outside the hotel to Tahiti Faa'a International Airport on the outskirts of Papeete. Two hours later he was airborne and spread out across three seats on the first leg of a half-empty night flight to Los Angeles. After dinner, the cabin lights were dimmed and Ewan sat in the dark slowly sipping his way through a Beaujolais miniature.

From his window seat at the back of the big A340 jetliner, he looked down on a Pacific Ocean amply bathed in the monochrome light of another stunning full moon. He smiled. For in his heart he knew that his grieving was ended.

EPILOGUE

After his farewell dinner with Ewan, Tom Morgate spent the next few days in Papeete deciding what best to do with *Bella Mama* in the wake of his wife's mysterious disappearance. The Swede and Pierre said they would be willing to continue the passage to New Zealand, as originally planned, if that was his wish. Some repairs needed to be undertaken before leaving Tahiti, but *Bella Mama* could certainly be in Auckland in time for the America's Cup. Morgate's other options were either to put the vessel up for sale in Tahiti -- where the market for used recreational craft was small -- or have her sailed back across the Pacific to the United States.

Having discussed the matter with family and friends in Illinois, the genial octogenarian decided – partly in memory of his late wife and partly from a desire to witness the great sailing event ahead – that *Bella Mama* should continue its passage to New Zealand. It had always been the plan to use her as a floating hotel and supporter vessel: draped in American flags and rooting for the US challenger. Lavinia's absence would obviously cast a sombre shadow over events. But under the circumstance, he felt it was the right thing to do.

Two weeks later -- all repairs having been completed -- *Bella Mama* set sail from Papeete early one morning bound for Auckland with a two-man crew – The Swede and Pierre -- on board. The Swede told Morgate that his course would be westwards to Cook Island, then to Tonga and -- time permitting -- on to Fiji. After that they would plot a course due south for the long passage to New Zealand.

Research later confirmed that the vessel had indeed received inbound clearance to Cook Island and, a week later, that she had been cleared by the immigration authorities out of Tonga. But that was the last that was ever heard or seen by Tom Moorgate or anyone else of *Bella Mama* and her intrepid two-man crew.